THE HAT

A KATE BRADY NOVEL

BABETTE HUGHES

A POST HILL PRESS book

ISBN (trade paperback): 978-1-61868-911-5
ISBN (eBook): 978-1-61868-912-2

The Hat (*A Kate Brady Novel*) copyright © 2015
by Babette Hughes
All Rights Reserved.
Cover art by Ryan Truso

Post Hill
PRESS

To Eric and Steve
Forever

I can calculate the movement of stars
But not the madness of men
Isaac Newton

CHAPTER 1
THE DAY OF THE MURDER

June 10, 1932

Ben Gold's killer knew that he was a man of regular habits. His bedroom light went on exactly at 7:00, the bathroom light at 7:10, and he was always nattily dressed in suit and fedora by 7:40 when he left for his morning walk to Jake's Newsstand to pick up the *Cleveland Plain Dealer*.

The killer also knew that Gold took a shortcut through a nearby alley and the killer waited there, hidden in a doorway of an indented and closed shoe repair shop. Sometimes, if a headline happened to interest Gold as he walked back with the newspaper, he would stop and read the article, which worried the assassin because it could dangerously throw the timing off. But in exactly five minutes, Gold's footsteps were heard. As he approached, the executioner removed the safety of the Smith & Wesson .38, stepped out, and pointed the gun. Small, dressed in knickers, a shirt and cap, the murderer looked to be no more than fifteen or sixteen years old.

Gold opened his mouth in puzzlement then in shocked recognition.

The bullet shattered Ben Gold's face.

Chapter 2
Two Years Before the Murder

April 10, 1930

Standing next to my mother I actually felt her vibrating nerves and great gin-thirst. And saw that the hat on her head was all wrong. The butler had led us through the elegant high-ceilinged rooms to the broad flower-bordered patio, and we stood there staring at the clusters of animated ladies and gentlemen in their perfect spring clothes, the terraced lawn and striped tent with the buffet table bearing trays of canapés, small sandwiches, pastel fruits, glistening pastries. Vivian's family had decided to have the party a month before graduation so as not to conflict with the other celebrations and events on their daughters' social calendars.

Two weeks earlier when I came home from school my mother had opened the door grinning from ear to ear. "We're invited to Vivian's graduation party!"

My heart sank. I had planned to get the invitation out of the mailbox before she got home from work. But all I said was, "Of course we're invited. She's inviting the whole graduation class."

"And their parents," she reminded me.

Which was what worried me. "Mama," I said, "your nerves. The party'll be bad for your nerves." Nerves was the word we'd used for her drinking since I was seven years old.

"Don't worry about my nerves."

"So why didn't you go to work today?"

"I had a headache."

Headache. We both knew what that meant. I watched my mother stand the engraved invitation up against the toaster. "Look. Mama—"

She turned to me, smiling. "Kate. I promise. I won't drink. I promise."

I shouldn't have believed her. But I loved my mother for the rigid sobriety she sometimes managed and was keenly aware of the discipline and loss it required. Like the times between binges when I came home from school and there'd be a gleaming apartment that smelled of soap, fragrant beef stew simmering on the stove, apple sauce, and yellow sponge cake cooling on the cracked enamel table, a perfectly sober, scrubbed, brushed, bustling, smiling, crisply-aproned mother, a mother from my most improbable fantasies. We would sit down to this normal dinner as if it was not at all out of the ordinary, as if this was the way we always lived and always would, and by the time I got into my sweet-smelling bed of freshly washed and ironed sheets I had come to believe it, reversing in my mind the real and the unreal mother; this mother was the real mom, the one who would stay; the drunk mother was a mistake, a terrible exception (now seemed rectified forever). The proof lay in my warm and full stomach and these very real, tight, clean sheets and the left-over stew and apple sauce in bowls in the ice box, all correctly covered with waxed paper.

As soon as Vivian saw me and my mother standing there staring, she rushed over, her blonde hair flying. "Kate! Mrs. Brady!" she cried. "You're so late!" She took my mother's hand. "Come, Mrs. Brady, I want you to meet my mom."

My mother stiffened and pulled back. Vivian and I had been best friends since seventh grade, but our mothers had never met. Although both happened to be Jewish, they were separated by money, class, background, and education—not to mention Mrs. Joseph's anti-Semitic social climbing. So what did Vivian think she was doing by dragging my mom over to meet her?

But she had her by the elbow and was half leading, half dragging her over to her mother, while I hurried along behind. Mrs. Joseph was standing with a group of four or five ladies in a chiffon dress to her ankles and a matching wide-brimmed hat. She was small, with dark hair and eyes, and a soft, round face—you would never think blonde Vivian with her cheekbones and height was her daughter. In fact, Vivian wanted to believe she wasn't, and not because of her looks. She thought her mother was a snob.

Mrs. Joseph said hello Kate or something like that and when Vivian introduced my mother she merely nodded with a sort of half smile and turned back to her friends. And that was that. I didn't know whether to be relieved or furious. Vivian was so flushed and excited by the party she didn't seem to notice how rudely Mrs. Joseph dismissed my mother, and was already pulling me over to the tent. I looked back helplessly at her standing alone in the middle of the lawn. I didn't want to leave my mother there.

But we joined Alice, Jessica, and Isobel—three of our classmates who had excluded us since seventh grade from their parties and homes and tennis courts and speedboats and summer picnics; from their lives.

Invitations had been sent and received for Isobel's coming out party but not by Vivian or me. For the others, Vivian may have been the first Jew they had ever seen, with or without horns. And she was certainly the first Jew ever permitted to cross the threshold of the rarefied environs of The Windsor Danbury School for Girls on its wooded Shaker Heights campus. That is, if you don't count a few distant Rothschild cousins and the three or four daughters of families who had changed their names and joined the Episcopal Church. And I was a scholarship student and probably the less said about my family the better. Being half Catholic and poor was the least of it—my Jewish mother had a "drinking problem"—as they called it in those days—and I hadn't seen my father, Nolan Brady, since he ran out on us when I was five. Vivian's paternal grandparents were the well-known philanthropists, Samson and Hilda Joseph, but for all I knew my grandparents were still in Ireland, or maybe they ran away somewhere, too. Maybe vanishing runs in the family. But equally rejected by our classmates in the politely cruel way of their privilege and upbringing, the vast differences between Vivian and me of money and family and religion and anything else you might name were leveled, and we became best friends. At Windsor Danbury, prejudice was a great leveler, as democratic as death.

"Kate, your dress is so pretty," Alice was saying.

"Thank you," I said, watching my mother out of the corner of my eye as she joined a group of three or four people on the lawn. Well, my dress should be pretty. It took maybe six months of wrapping bagels and cholla bread and Kaiser rolls at Shapiro's Bakery. But it *was* pretty; a sheer white cotton with a wide off-the-shoulder ruffle and another one along the hem.

"Did you get the scholarship?" Isobel asked me.

"It came last week," I said, grinning, glad she asked.

"What's your major?"

"English."

Isobel nodded. "I liked your stories you read in class."

"I'm, going to be a writer," I said. I didn't tell her that I had no idea where I'd get the money for room and board and books.

It seemed as if I had been waiting all my life to leave home. Or anyway, since I was maybe six, after my father took off. And by the time I was fourteen I was afraid that if I didn't get away I'd start acting like my mother. Watching her relax happily with her bourbon over ice I sometimes envied her this sweet oblivion, and these wistful impulses scared me. Smiling a half smile, as if listening to something enticing, like music or a lover, my mother sipped proudly with her pinky finger sticking out, tinkling the ice she had chipped off the big block in the icebox. Her fingers caressed the glass, actually caressed its cool, moist surface slowly, as if she loved it. Well, she did love it. More than me. No doubt about it. I could never make her feel that good.

I walked around the buffet table sampling a small chicken sandwich and a strange-tasting canapé, with one eye on my mother. The people she had been with were drifting away, and I watched as she went over to the silver punch bowl and helped herself to a cupful. She stood sipping, looking around with a soft, attentive smile on her face. The waiter passing canapés offered her his tray. She studied the assortment and chose one, holding it daintily. No one was talking to her or anything and she stood alone on the sweeping lawn looking small and alert. I wanted to go over to her, but Isobel was watching me narrowly and I felt a familiar stab of shame. I was ashamed of my mother—of her dress of lilacs on a brown background and the hat on her head and her periodic binges and her job setting hair and the flask of bootlegged gin she carried around in her purse. I felt my face get hot. I was ashamed of being ashamed.

"Congratulations," Alice was saying. "My sister graduated from State last year. She liked it okay."

"On a scholarship?" Vivian asked.

"Not with her grades," she said, giggling. Alice was the first one to grow breasts that showed. There had been a rumor that she was actually engaged to someone, but Isobel, who knew everything, said the rumor was rubbish, and that the new and enormous star sapphire ring she wore on her left hand was actually a graduation gift from her parents. Even though everyone knew that Alice was so rich she could probably marry just about anyone, I couldn't imagine how a rumor like that could have started—the only contact we were permitted with boys was at the chaperoned dances at University School with pimply-faced, sweaty, skinny boys who were too short and pressed their hard thing against you during the fox trot.

"Is your mother here?" Isobel asked me.

"She's around somewhere," I answered, waving my arm vaguely. But when I looked I couldn't see her. Trying not to panic I walked among the clusters of guests, checking out the buffet table and punch bowl. My mother had vanished.

I found Vivian and pulled her aside. "Have you seen my mother?"

"Stop worrying about her for once. We're at my party. She's okay. Maybe she went to the bathroom or something. Relax." She took my arm. "Come on, let's get some punch."

Vivian's right, I told myself. Relax, I told myself. We went over to the punch bowl and Vivian filled two cups. Then we joined our classmates again and I stood there, holding a glass cup of pink punch, pretending I had a regular mother. Isobel, Jessica, and Alice were talking about spending the July Fourth weekend at Alice's hunting lodge in Virginia, continuing their conversation as if Vivian and I were not standing there, uninvited. Suddenly, I didn't care. Not anymore. I had graduated from their mean world.

"Is that your mother?" Isobel asked, gesturing. Looking up, I saw her come out of the house and weave unsteadily toward one of the waiters. While I watched, while they all watched, she took a glass of punch off his tray, poured some gin into it from her flask, and drained it. Then she took a swig directly from the flask. Of course. That's where she'd been. Drinking in the house, probably the bathroom. My hands started to sweat. I knew how little it took to get my mother thoroughly drunk. She now had a passionate grip on the white-coated waiter while he tried valiantly to disengage himself from her fist on his lapel.

When I could get my legs to move, I dashed over and got hold of her arm. "Mama," I said, "let's go."

"Get away from me!" she hollered. Then she said to someone over my shoulder, "Who the hell you think you're staring at?"

I turned around. Vivian's mother was standing in a halo of chiffon, a small woman, really, who looked as if she packed more wallop in her hundred plus pounds and five feet two frame than any man, woman or beast twice her size. She had a presence, a stature that imposed itself, no doubt about it. And here she was looking at my mother as if from Mt. Olympus, short as she was. And she was definitely not pleased.

"I think you'd better get your mother home," Mrs. Joseph said to me. Her voice was soft. It also had the steel command of a field general.

"I heard you!" my mother yelled. "I heard what you said! Who the hell you think you're sending home!" she hollered. I grabbed her arm but she jerked it away so hard she spilled her drink, just missing Mrs. Joseph's chiffon. "You listen to me! Katie and me we're not goin' home. Katie and me we're staying right here at this here party!" My mother drew herself up with great dignity. "Me and my daughter we're just as goddamn good as you and so's my daughter!" she shouted, waving her hand around that held the flask. Some of the gin spilled on my dress. I smelled it. The entire party had stopped, everyone on the lawn and under the tent staring motionlessly as if frozen in a photograph. Even my own legs seemed nailed to the ground, and I do not know how I got my mother to the street. Even later, all I could remember were the staring young ladies in their white graduation dresses and my own flaming face and wet eyes.

Somehow I got her on the streetcar and home. Inside the apartment my mother walked to her bed skillfully skirting the couch and ironing board with her hand outstretched like a dignified blind person. Although she rarely stumbled or tripped in her path from her drinking chair, as I'd called it since I was ten years old, I took my usual position behind her until she had passed out safely on her bed.

CHAPTER 3

Although President Hoover assured the country that prosperity was just around the corner, the fact was that so many customers were being laid off they only bought day-old bread, and Mrs. Shapiro had to let Mr. Ornstein go, get up in the middle of the night, and do the baking herself. And I was next. Three months after Vivian and her trunks left for Pembroke College, Mrs. Shapiro put her arms around me and told me with wet eyes that Friday would have to be my last day. When I began to feel tears gather behind my eyes, I swallowed them back—I felt as if I had somehow accumulated a reservoir of tears that lay ancient and unshed from before history, and I was afraid if I let go and started crying I would never stop. I had to keep my finger in the dike.

But my eyes kept filling up anyway and I was still wiping them on my apron and Mrs. Shapiro was blowing her nose like a foghorn, when Ben Gold strode into the bakery. He asked Mrs. Shapiro for a loaf of rye and stood staring at me while she wrapped it. Snapping the string smartly, Mrs. Shapiro took his money and handed him his bread and change, but instead of leaving with his bread under his arm as he usually did, he walked over to me and stretched his hand across the counter. "Ben Gold," he said with his splendid smile.

"Kate Brady," I said, taking his hand.

"Would you let me see you home some time?" he asked, smiling.

But I was too shaken to speak. Where was I to find another job when the newspapers were full of the threat of plant closings and foreclosures? This morning's *Plain Dealer* had an article about the fear of actual hunger and soup lines. What was I going to do? The person I had trusted above all else since I was ten years old had just fired me. The sweet smell of coconut bars and macaroons lined up on the counter was making me sick. My life was making me sick. The scholarship I was about to lose was making me sick. Vivian was gone. Everyone else I knew from school was scattered and were never my friends anyway. I had no idea what to do after Friday or with the rest of my life, and I felt such an appalling convulsion of rage and grief that the floor seemed to move under my feet. I held onto the counter. Aware that this Ben Gold was standing there smiling at me, I began wiping the display case again and told him that I wouldn't be coming to work after Friday.

"So how about today? I sure do waste a lot of bread on account of you, Kate Brady," he said, grinning. "That's a shame in times like these. And it's all your fault."

Of course I had noticed him come into the bakery for days staring at me while Mrs. Shapiro wrapped his bread and counted out the change in his palm. But that stored-up avalanche of tears was threatening me again, and all I could do was wonder what on earth he saw in me that kept him coming back for bread he didn't want in such desperate times. Just fired by my mentor, the kind, deep-voiced widow Shapiro, unemployed and unwanted and nowhere to go, I felt too thin, my hair too curly and red and unfashionably long, my skin too white, my eyes too pale, not to mention the haughty manner that inspired Mrs. Shapiro to call me the Queen of Sheba. (Don't forget Mrs. Robbins owes for three loaves, Miss Queen of Sheba; or the front case needs cleaning today, Miss Queen of Sheba, she would say when she left for her coffee and corned beef sandwich at Feldman's Delicatessen each afternoon at one.)

"Cat got your tongue?" Ben said, smiling. I looked up at him. He was wearing a tan double-breasted suit, pale mesh wing tips, a yellow shirt and a tie of pastel paisley, topped off with a skimmer. A winter sun dappled his dark hair and pastel hues with light and shadow; his amber eyes had golden lights, which (I learned later) upon certain occasions of anger or other inner heat would actually turn yellow. He reminded me of a movie star, Rudolph Valentino or John Barrymore, someone like that. Staring at his gallant and exotic appearance only moments after I lost everything suddenly had for me the magic of a fairy tale and I had a swift seductive fantasy of rescue. I did not know then that self-deception is the child of confusion and pain; I breathed the air of sentimental delusion as if this smiling stranger was a hand pulling me back from the edge, and I flirted back as if I were Joan Crawford in the movies, or deep in a sweet daydream.

But I couldn't let him take me home. My mother embarrassed me. It was as if her years of drinking had eaten a permanent rut of shame within my heart, leaving it like a damaged liver. A casual reference to my mother by someone could still make my heart stop with mortification as if they knew about all the times Mr. Blum called the school office with a message that my mother was spending my father's occasional check in Blum's Grocery Store on unlikely assortments: five jars of Hellman's mayonnaise and six loaves of Wonder Bread, or eight tins of red domestic caviar, or a dozen cans of Tabby Cat Food (we had no cat) and a bag of onions, among other fanciful combinations. Once she bought nothing but six cabbages.

The monitor would hand me the folded note, and face flaming, I'd slip out of class feeling the weight of my mother's failings as my own. After riding the streetcar to my neighborhood, I would walk toward Blum's as slowly as I could, looking over my shoulder, my heart pounding with a terrible humiliation and an appalling fury that seemed to hold the very bones in my feet captive. I would usually find my mother halfway home by now, cradling her grocery bag to her breast like a baby and trailing her familiar gin-smell. She made the watching neighbors feel, I knew, superior and virtuous, in spite of their own bottle kept discretely under the sink with the Brillo pads and scouring powder; in spite of the roll they would swipe from the open bin (I saw them) when Mrs. Shapiro wasn't looking.

But my mother was on the wagon now, and if I brought Ben home she would change into her polished white shoes with the Cuban heels and put on her best dress—a print of small lilacs on a brown background. My mother would make tea and arrange fig newtons and ginger snaps from their boxes in neat rows on a scalloped paper doily. She would talk about the weather and look apprehensive and distracted, and her hands would tremble the way they never did when she drank, and I would not be able to understand my own confused and guilty rage, or why I felt so wretched.

"So, how about it?" Ben was saying.

Blushing from this dapper stranger's persistent attention, feeling moist from the heat of the ovens and my own blush and the unseasonably warm November afternoon, I saw Ben Gold's car through the storefront window, a shining black Packard. Except for Vivian's parents no one I knew had an automobile, not even Mrs. Shapiro.

Mrs. Shapiro got up from her stool where she had been sitting pretending not to listen. She opened the cash register and handed me my week's wages of eight dollars. "Go," she said, giving me a hard little shove. "I'm closing up early."

I took off my apron. "Let's go over to Hansen's," I said to Ben Gold.

* * *

The next day I told my mother I was going job-hunting and took the streetcar downtown to meet Ben for lunch, as we had arranged when we sat drinking lemonade in a torn booth in Hansen's Coffee Shop. It was the warmest November on record, the radio said, and from the streetcar window I watched stray newspapers tossed about by an unseasonably warm wind. Inside, people in their seats pulled off coats and stared out on the bare winter trees, looking uneasy.

Ben was waiting for me when I arrived at Halle's Department Store, slouched against the glove counter, looking around in that observant, arrogant way of his. From the pearl-gray wide-brimmed fedora on his head to his brown wingtips, he looked as if he owned the place. I looked down at my cotton blouse, plaid skirt, and the coat over my arm and thought about the beautiful clothes Vivian's mother bought her for college. I imagined the feel of silk on my skin, the way Vivian's blue chiffon prom dress would look with my hair. Damn. When Ben saw me he flashed his grand smile, and without speaking, took my arm and steered me past the cosmetic counter out the door to his car at the curb. The knot of people who had gathered around the car scattered while the doorman sprinted ahead, opened the door, and handed me inside.

When we arrived at the restaurant, Mr. and Mrs. Wong greeted us with smiles and bows and Mrs. Wong led us through the nearly-empty restaurant to a white-clothed table next to a window. Ben ordered grandly, seriously. First there was egg drop soup, then egg foo yong, chop suey, chow mein, thin crispy noodles, rice, tea in tiny cups, and almond cookies. Ben sat quietly across the table from me, but I felt his presence powerfully. There was something melodramatic about my attraction to Ben—as if he were someone in the movies, someone unreal, someone you made up because you didn't have a job or a boyfriend. Years later, there were times when I thought he was in the next room or with me in the dark. Sometimes I imagined his breath on my cheek.

Ben talked while I ate, eating little himself, speaking rapidly, as if trying to cover much material in a short time, as if he had to rush off to another appointment. (I noticed him glance at his watch.) He said he was twenty-eight years old, that he had started his own insurance business when he was eighteen and built it up during the boom years. He told me that when everyone else was riding the stock market he took his father's advice and sewed his money in the mattress. He was now buying properties all over town at a fraction of their value, he said, as well as gold and diamonds. He had two employees, an accountant, and a general helper who served as driver, premium collector, errand runner, and whatever else had to be done, and they all worked from offices in his house.

I told him about school and about my scholarship and about Mrs. Shapiro. I told him that I didn't know where my father was and that my mother used to work at Irene's Beauty Shop setting her customers' hair in the latest style. But my mother was an invalid now, I told him, needed me home to take care of her, and didn't want me to go away to college or out on dates. I don't know why I lied. Ben listened with a kind of amused attentiveness as if he knew I was lying. His fingernails were shiny and immaculate, his hair was clipped and brushed, and he smelled of a pine forest.

After lunch we drove out of the city toward the Heights. I opened the window and let the wind blow my hair back—the only time I got to ride in an automobile was when Vivian's chauffeur picked her up at school on rainy days and gave me a lift home. As we drove into Vivian's neighborhood, the houses grew larger, more elegant, and farther apart; the trees taller and grander, the lawns mysteriously weedless. Even the shrubs were as perfectly shaped as on a child's board game. Order and tranquility seemed to float from the proud silent streets into the car and the fragrant breeze I felt on my face, like the invisible people who lived here, never seemed to come to my neighborhood. There were no signs of children or dogs or dirt, as if the houses weren't for real people at all, just facades on a movie set.

Ben slowed the car as we approached a large red brick house with white pillars that reminded me of pictures I had seen of antebellum Southern mansions. It was set back from the street and almost hidden by a range of viburnums and rhododendrons. He pulled the car into the circular driveway, came around to my side of the car, and opened the door.

I sat on the soft white leather seat staring straight ahead.

"Come on in," he said. "I want to show you my house."

I didn't budge.

"Come on," he said again, smiling, his urgency crackling the air. "I don't bite."

"I have to be getting home."

He slammed the door, got back behind the wheel, and started the car.

"It's just that my mother's strict," I said, wishing it were true.

He drove without speaking, fists on the steering wheel. His obvious intentions and my own excitement that escalated with his heated presence bothered me and I moved over to the window. I glanced at his flushed profile. He was no longer a safe distance across a lunch table, no longer a romantic idea of rescue. He was too real, too old for me, too sure of himself; I was in over my head and I knew it. He would take me home and I would never see him again.

But I did not want to go home. My mother was there, clattering around in the unlaced oxfords that she wore two sizes too large to accommodate the big bunions that rose like pink marbles from her crooked disfigured toes. This was from her years of working in the Chinese laundry over on Chapman Street. This was before she drank, before I remembered. The klopity noise my mother always made on the thin rug in her oversized shoes was a familiar sound to me from early childhood, a comfort, telling me that my mother was near. Remembering how I longed to be near my mother then, it was impossible to believe how much I longed to be away from her now.

My mother had been pretty once; in the mornings when she was fresh, after she did up her hair, if I squinted my eyes I could see beyond the ruined face to her chiseled features and wide extravagantly blue eyes. Or I could look at the photograph of her at the age of fourteen on the wall. She is standing second from the right between her sisters, behind her seated parents and brothers, all of them staring out of their sepia tones at my half-Catholic self with their virtuous, grave Jewish faces. The father, his hands on his thighs, has a splendid mustache and my own pale eyes; the mother has tightly combed hair and sits severely in a high-necked dress stretched over a weighty bosom. (My mother's wedding picture, which I only dimly remembered, had been removed long ago, leaving a neat, pale square on the wall.) Even at fourteen my mother's prettiness was clearly defined, but later, when I knew her, drinking, or at night when she was tired, her hair hanging down long and gray, her skin the color of putty, she looked bad to me, like a witch, and it seemed dangerous to look at her. So I fastened my eyes on her bosom, level with my eyes then; later, her breasts seemed to sort of disappear, but back then they were fleshy and voluptuous.

That face reminded me of the relief I felt when my mother left for her first day of work at Irene's Beauty Shop and the hopelessness that followed an instant later when I saw the empty gin bottle in the waste basket from the night before. And of the way my mother stood so straight when she was drinking that she tilted slightly backward. And of the time she decided to make my clothes. (She did things like that.) She sat in the light, humming to herself, looking maternal and virtuous, sewing an entire dress by hand, ordering me to turn this way and that with a motherly, bossy frown. I stood patiently for the fittings, glad to have a regular normal mother who sewed. The dress, flowered chiffon with a stiff collar that scratched my neck, was meant for the Christmas dance but was never finished. By that time my mother was drinking again and didn't notice that I didn't go.

Thinking about my mother made me want to sit next to Ben, and I slid over on the seat until our bodies touched.

He looked at me. "So when will Mama let you out again?"

"Tomorrow?"

"I'll pick you up at eight."

"No, tomorrow afternoon."

"You can't go out at night?"

"I'll meet you at Halle's glove counter again. Same time," I said, too much my own parent for too long to drop my guard. I got out of the car at the bakery and watched it roar away. Later I wondered about losing my job and meeting Ben within minutes, as if all the while I thought I was making choices, there were cunning, mysterious forces out there planning the life I would have.

Walking home, the cool November air seemed somehow menacing, as if seasonably cold streets belonged only to the employed. No one else was on the sidewalk, only an occasional car rumbled by, the streetcar tracks were abandoned; there was only silence and a cloudless sky. Where was everyone? It was just past four o'clock and yet the forsaken neighborhood and motionless air seemed to be trapped in a sealed bottle like a preserved and lifeless specimen shimmering in an eerie light. I passed the tailor shop and saw Mr. Haefner, alone in his store, bending over his sewing machine, but next door, Oscar's Fresh Fish was darkened and empty, a big hand-lettered OUT OF BUSINESS sign propped up on an empty milk bottle in the window. As I passed Feldman's Delicatessen, the tantalizing smell of pickles and pastrami drifted out into the street, but inside, the tables were empty and Mr. Feldman's son, Arnold, was slowly mopping the floor.

Just ahead a line of men stood as quietly as obedient children waiting their turn at the new soup kitchen that had been Blum's Grocery Store. Some men wore heavy black suits. Some wore hats. Were the careworn expressions on their cleanly-shaved faces under the brave fedoras a final humiliation? The fear in their sagging bodies and gray faces seemed to emit a stench and I hurried past, averting my eyes as if they were naked.

I had never been on a regular date before—just the dances at University School, or an after-school coke with Tommy Leblanc, and the afternoons when Vivian and I and a bunch of kids from the public school squeezed into Frieda Norton's living room and played spin the bottle until Frieda's mother was laid off and was home after school. I was relieved when we had to quit because Harvey Rheinhart always pressed his lips too hard against my teeth and tried to get his hand in my blouse. But Ben was good looking and polite; we went for country rides after our lunches, and then to Schrafft's for a soda before he drove me back to my street corner. Sometimes we went to the movies. I didn't become suspicious of his grand attentions and gentlemanly behavior.

It was a sexless deliverance I wanted back then, like when the movie star still had her clothes on before disappearing behind the closed door with the man, before the camera averted its eye toward the sunset. When I was nine or ten I remembered hearing a man's voice from my bed at night, laughter, the clinking of ice in glasses. The next day my mother looked younger, prettier, as pretty as the picture on the wall. Even then I recognized the signs. The extra whisky glass. The rose he brought her. The scent of a male mixed with the sort of flowery gentility my mother had in those days. Once there was a whole bouquet in a vase; he was a sport, my mother said. The man was always gone when I got up the next morning and I wondered if maybe he was married or something. But I pretended my mother didn't let him stay because of me. I was relieved when he stopped coming and my mother started to look old again.

Chapter 4

When Ben drove me back to my street corner after our third or fourth afternoon together, he grabbed my hand as I reached for the door handle and leaned over to kiss me.

"Ben, it's broad daylight," I said, pushing him away.

"So come out tonight."

"I can't."

"Why not?"

"I told you."

"Yeah. Your mama's strict." His hand shot across me and jerked the door open so violently I was afraid he was going to push me out of the car. Looking back, if I could have found one moment when I chose a road or burned a bridge it was then, sitting next to Ben with the car door open. I did not get out of the car and slam the door in his red face. I sat there imagining his power to save me and thought it was love. I put my hand on his fist. "Don't be mad, Ben."

He turned off the motor and looked at me. "Do you want to see me again?"

"Yes, tomorrow." I kissed him lightly on the lips. He was so surprised, and I was out of the car before he could reach me.

I wrote Vivian at Pembroke about the fabulous man who was giving me this big rush. She wrote back saying she was dying to meet him and would visit me during Christmas break. Perfectly aware of how her parents must have objected, I had to be grateful for the two days she promised me.

Vivian's total absence from my life had left a gap I felt daily. Besides, you could hardly call my life exactly interesting—except for my afternoons with Ben I seemed to be more or less drifting, reading the want ads, going to employment agencies looking for jobs I didn't want that weren't there anyway, working my mother's jigsaw puzzle. Jigsaw puzzles were my mother's other addiction, but she never seemed to stay on the wagon long enough to finish one, and the pastoral scene broken up over the top of our wobbly card table was as much a permanent part of our living room as the ironing board and sagging couch.

By the time Vivian's visit finally rolled around, I had worked myself up into a pretty good state of excitement. Her train was due at 9 AM on Thursday, December 14. She would spend the morning with her parents, Vivian wrote, meet Ben and me for lunch, and then go home with me. She had wrangled two more days from her mother and father she said, and could stay the weekend. I was ecstatic. Four days! Ben picked Schrafft's for our lunch and I wrote Vivian to meet us there at one o'clock.

It had been snowing earlier that day, but while I dressed the clouds passed, and as I left the apartment to meet Ben a winter sun was melting the snow into fast little streams on the sidewalk. There was a pitiful Christmas wreath on the door of our apartment building but the neighborhood merchants had draped a row of pretty little red and green lights across the street at the stop sign, and there was a beautiful glittering Christmas tree in the window of Allen's Drug Store.

Vivian was already waiting for Ben and me when we pulled up in front of Schrafft's Restaurant. Sick of feeling like a poor relation, I was pleased that Vivian saw me sitting in Ben's Packard. But I was proud of Vivian, too, standing there with her valise, looking beautiful in a blue wool fox-trimmed suit and brimmed sailor hat and those fabulous bones. She could have been a photographer's model if she wanted to—which she didn't. Once when we were in ninth grade, the fashion director of Halle's came to Windsor Danbury to pick girls to model in a teen fashion show. She made a beeline for Vivian, who turned red as a beet and vigorously shook her head. The woman picked me, too, but I had to work at the bakery Saturdays. I was disappointed, but what the hell. I would have hated giving the clothes back anyway.

I introduced my best friend and Ben proudly, at that moment feeling better, happier, than I had since Mrs. Shapiro fired me. Ben gave Vivian his dazzling smile, but just as Vivian extended her gloved hand, a short, muscular man appeared out of nowhere at Ben's side.

"I been waitin' for you," he said to Ben. He seemed agitated. "Sam told me—"

Ben got hold of his arm and hurried him away while Vivian and I stood waiting in front of the restaurant. Ben and the man spoke intensely for a few minutes and then he left as abruptly as he had arrived.

"I'm sorry," Ben said when he came back. "Business." He grinned at Vivian. "And just when I'm trying to make a good impression on Kate's best friend."

We were greeted effusively by the headwaiter and ushered grandly to the best table in the restaurant. Feeling a delicious little stab of vicarious power, I looked sideways at Vivian to see if she had noticed

Ben's grand entrance, but she was clearly unimpressed, staring straight ahead with her mother's imperious expression. She kept that infuriating look on her face all during lunch in spite of Ben's smiles and attention and the elaborate way he ordered for the three of us—shrimp cocktails, Welsh rarebit, a Schrafft's specialty. Salads of artichokes and tomatoes. Popovers, fresh from the oven. Vivian picked at her food and scarcely spoke while I found myself gobbling mine down and chattering like a birdbrain to fill the silence. This was not going well. Not at all. It puzzled me. We all refused dessert and coffee. Ben asked for the check. Everyone seemed relieved. He held Vivian's chair politely, then mine, and helped us on with our coats. In the car on the way home, I kept up my stupid chatter until we arrived at my apartment and climbed out of the car. Ben carried Vivian's valise to the front door, Vivian said her thanks in her mother's voice, and he got back into the Packard and roared away.

The weather had turned nasty with wet snow and an icy wind blowing down from Canada, and Vivian shivered, hugging herself. Can a person be too bewildered and disappointed over a miserable lunch to even feel the cold? Because I didn't. I was hot.

Vivian had been in my apartment so many times over the years I was surprised at the stab of embarrassment I felt at the smells and shabby light that confronted us. Watching her stand in the middle of the stuffed little living room, pulling off her gloves, all I could smell was my mother's sauerkraut and gin and all I could think of was the watery soup and hard potatoes and the pasty macaroni and cheese my mother had always served us for Saturday lunches. The Josephs' cook gave us chicken sandwiches, hamburgers, rice pudding, homemade ice cream (only when Mrs. Joseph was out, I realized later). And their house smelled of piney furniture polish and bread baking and the fresh roses that always stood on a marble pedestal in the foyer. Then these differences didn't seem to have anything to do with Vivian and me. Now, looking at Vivian in the living room as she slowly pulled off her gloves, the differences in our lives seemed to turn into an abyss.

"Okay, Vivian," I said, tossing off my coat. "Out with it. What's wrong?"

"That man? Ben's friend? Outside the restaurant? He's one of those union thugs!"

"Vivian, I haven't the faintest idea what you're talking about."

She started talking in a rush, something about her father hiring scabs when his cutters and pressers went on strike. She said that Ben's friend came to her house that morning. She knew it was the same man because she let him in. He talked to her father in the library with the door closed, and when he left, her father told her that he had threatened to have the scabs wiped out if he didn't fire them. She said her father refused and ordered him out. "Then Daddy got a phone call that the scabs were beat up! Two died!" She looked at me intently. "Listen. Listen to me. These goons were just waiting with baseball bats and iron pipes for a phone call from that man after my father ordered him out," she went on, speaking slowly, distinctly, as if I were retarded or hard of hearing or something. She got up and paced our small living room, back and forth, back and forth. "That man? Talking to Ben in front of the restaurant? My God, Kate, he's a murderer!"

"You're mistaken. That wasn't him."

"It *was* him! I saw him!" she said, running her fingers through her hair. She had just had one of those fashionable, short, boyish bobs that I thought made her look sort of pin-headed. Breathing hard, she sat down again.

Even sitting down, she seemed to fill the apartment more than my mother and me put together. The length of her legs, or the fur on her suit, or her blonde elegance seemed to push at the walls, reminding me painfully of these small, meager rooms and my small, meager life. "Well, even if it was him, Ben didn't have anything to do with it," I told her. "Ben's in the insurance business."

Vivian gave me a level look. "You can judge a person by the company he keeps," she said in that tone I had heard her mother use to the cook.

"You sound just like your mother," I said. That always got a rise out of her.

"I do not!" she said, glaring at me.

"I'm sorry," I said, pleased. It was true. Even that level look. I went into the kitchen. I didn't want to hear any more of this stuff.

"How long have you known him?" Vivian called.

"Do you want some coffee?"

"No!"

"Tea?"

"Kate, will you please come out of there?"

As I came back into the living room, Vivian was standing up and tossing off her suit jacket. "It's too hot in here."

She was right about that. Mornings you could freeze to death, but every day at three o'clock the radiators sizzled and banged making you sweat.

Vivian tried to get the window open.

"Forget it," I told her. "It's stuck."

Vivian sat down smoothing her hair. "I asked you," she said again. "How long have you known him?"

I shrugged. "Not long."

"Not long. Like maybe a couple of weeks?" Vivian started chewing on her thumbnail. She did that whenever she got upset, since she was twelve years old. "You're eighteen, for God's sake. How old is he? Thirty?" she said wearily, as if I were beyond redemption, an impossible case.

"Twenty-eight."

"Twenty-eight. Swell."

Part of what I liked about my dates with Ben was imagining how I would tell Vivian about him as we did at school when we chewed over our schoolgirl crushes. But Vivian seemed different to me now, as if she were leaving me behind somewhere. Later, much later, I understood. Vivian was growing up and I wasn't.

"Didn't you notice?" I said, grinning. "In the restaurant? The way everybody fussed over him?"

"Maybe they're afraid he'll get them killed with a baseball bat."

I wanted to shake her until her teeth rattled. I wanted to push her down with my fists. I slammed into my bedroom, a small island of order in the mess my mother, drunk or sober, left in her wake. It was where I studied and slept and read and could close the door to my mother. I took off the navy blue dress I had bought for Ohio State before I got fired.

"Please, Kate, don't get upset," Vivian called. "It's for your own good."

I groaned loudly. "For my own good. Yes, sir, you're your mama's daughter all right."

I had listened to Vivian complain about her mother since seventh grade. Which amused me, because when it came to mothers I was the one with plenty to criticize, and I never did. Rebelling against my mother was like fighting a shadow—what was the use? Besides, the way I saw it the only thing that stood between me and total terrifying orphanhood was my flawed and fragile mother, who somehow always managed to be there. Sort of. Sometimes. More or less. Anyway, I wasn't about to pick on her. I felt this kind of weird loyalty. I had to take care of her.

Vivian came into my room drinking water from one of the jelly jars we used for glasses. "He's too old for you and too, too—"

"Too sexy? What's the matter, Viv, jealous?"

Vivian turned on her heel and left the room. "Just hold on to that temper of yours, Kate," she said in a ragged voice.

I followed Vivian in my slip. "What would you have me do?" I said as quietly as I could. "Sit home with my mommy? Wait for prince charming? Or pennies from heaven? Or maybe you think an angel will come down from the sky and send me to college? Is that what you expect?"

"But a man like that—"

"A man like that can give me a better life than the one I've got."

"You mean you'd marry him?"

I stared at her. Our faces were inches apart. "You bet," I said, surprising myself. "If he'll have me."

"Now, Kate, wait a minute, don't go jumping from the frying pan into the fire—"

That did it. "Who the hell are you to talk about frying pans and fires!?"

Vivian's face turned red. She looked as full of guilt as if my bad luck was her fault. Anyway, I hoped so. In that mean moment I wanted her to be ashamed of her good fortune, her wealth, her sober parents, her closet full of clothes, her semesters at Pembroke. So I finished it off. "Don't you dare tell me what to do with my life while you go sailing off into the sunset!" I heard myself scream. "Just mind your own goddamn business!"

Vivian stared at me with brimming eyes. Her face was still red. She grabbed her jacket, slammed out of the apartment, and was gone. I stood there in my slip, too full of self-pity and confusion and anger to realize that in my disarray I saw Ben Gold as my only way out, and that I had to kill the messenger.

* * *

The following Monday Ben and I met at our usual place at Halle's glove counter. I expected him to say something about Vivian, maybe that she didn't seem to like him or something. But he didn't, and I didn't bring it up. I didn't want to think about Vivian.

After lunch he drove directly to his house and pulled into the circular driveway.

"Come on in, Kate."

I looked at him.

"Just for a minute," he said. "That's all, I promise. Just to see my house."

"Well, just for a minute."

Ben hurried ahead, unlocked the door, and I stepped into a long curtained room of velvets and brocades, mirrored walls and golden cupids that seemed to float in a liquid light. The slanting afternoon sun filtered through the sheer yellow draperies, shining the golden air. (Months later, the room looked to me as pristinely perfect and carefully cheerful as a funeral home.)

He waited until I had stared at the silken draperies, felt the shimmering fringe on the lamp shades, studied the ivory butterflies in their glass and mirrored cabinet, run my fingers up the white grand piano keyboard, tried out the blue brocaded chair with my feet up on the footstool. Then I was on the yellow velvet couch, Ben on top of me, feeling his tongue thrust in my mouth, his hot breath on my face, his hand on my breast, the hard swelling of his groin jammed against my thigh. When his hands began to fumble with the buttons on my dress, I put my fists on his chest and pushed. He reached under my dress to my garter belt and with fast, practiced fingers unfastened my stockings. His lust did not seem to have anything to do with me; it was quick as lightning, hot and direct, without sentiment. His fluent, moist mouth, his tenaciously moving hands, his body weight, his smell of heat, were fused into expert instruments of arousal, and I felt myself being thickly transported by his anonymity, his princely authority, his command. It excited me. Expanding with unknown flesh under his expert hands and hot breath, I wanted to follow the tidal promise of my lifting body without responsibility, an object. But suspended on the threshold of discovery, of fusing shuddering pleasure, I stopped. Something stopped me. I did not know if it was from my father's Catholic belief of sin, or a revelation of my own dangerous passion. Or if I knew in some ancient, mysterious instinct of feminine survival that if I didn't stop him I wouldn't get him to marry me. I pushed him with my hands and both knees. I pushed and pushed, until panting, he rolled off.

"You promised," I said, sounding like a child even to myself.

Breathing hard, Ben pulled his tie down. "I don't know why I put up with this."

I stood up. My stockings slid down to my ankles. I turned away and fastened them to my garters with trembling fingers.

Ben got up, taking his time. "Okay Kate," he said, turning to me with a small smile, "you won this one. But you're on notice." He straightened his tie, tugged at the points of his vest, and put on his suit jacket. "I always get what I want."

But I got what I wanted, too. I didn't know then that what I thought was true power was really only sexual power with its potential to be either Eros or the Angel of Death.

CHAPTER 5

The night before my wedding I dreamed of a woman, transparent and boneless and fluid as water, walking through walls, houses. I saw that it was Vivian. She was wearing a beautiful white satin bridal gown with a long train and there was a man with her who looked like either my father or Ben Gold. Or maybe both. In my dream I couldn't tell. I was watching them from Shapiro's Bakery in my Windsor Danbury uniform feeling sad. When I woke my cheeks were wet.

After my mother wished me luck on my wedding day, I arrived at City Hall early for our four-thirty ceremony. But Ben was already there, standing at the top of the steps near the heavy carved doors. He was wearing a dark coat. Two men were with him, one blond and very slim, the other thick and dark. From a distance, the dark one made me think of the man who used to bring my father home in the middle of the night, stumbling in his heavy shoes. I noticed that although Ben was wearing a fedora, the dark one had a yarmulke on his head. Looking at these strangers, I thought of how Vivian and I had solemnly promised to be each other's Maid Of Honor at our weddings. Missing her powerfully, I was ashamed, and in my shame and regret I tried to put her out of my mind. I tried to pretend she was dead.

I felt a chill and had a sudden impulse to turn around and go home. But I stood there on the bottom step curling my toes in my new beige high-heeled shoes, watching Ben and the two strangers come toward me as if in slow motion. While I waited the sky moved, startling me, but it was only a cloud passing over the sun.

Ben kissed my cheek and whispered in my ear, "How's my bride?" Then he gestured to the dark one. "This is my good right hand, Sam Ginsburg."

"Hello, Kate," Sam said, holding out his small hairy hand.

"And this is Bobby," Ben said.

"Robert Joseph Keane, at your service," said the other one, grinning. He was half a head taller than Ben, shined and polished from his parted blond wavy hair to his immaculate, shining fingernails, gleaming patent leather shoes, and gray spats. A gold watch chain was draped across his vest. He was the most elegant man I had ever seen. Not that Ben wasn't elegant in his own way, too, I told myself. Well, maybe not exactly elegant, but magnetic and honey-tongued when he wanted to be.

Ben, Sam, and Bobby all wore white carnations in their lapels. Smiling, Ben opened the box he was holding and pinned the corsage of white orchids to my suit. Even years later, in spite of everything that happened, I could remember the way Ben's sudden grin transformed his face that day, catching me like a tidal wave in its energy. His smile was the first thing I had noticed when he came into the bakery that day, and its heat and light caused a rising flutter somewhere in my midsection. In those days I saw wistfulness in Ben that just missed actual sweetness. But then he could turn away so abruptly with eyes so suddenly cold and flat it was as if he slammed a door in my baffled face. But now he was pinning orchids to my shoulder and smiling into my eyes. It was our wedding day.

The four of us found our way into a large office with green painted walls and rows of filing cabinets. The room smelled vaguely of paper and the perfume of previous brides. And food. Someone's lunch. I heard a typewriter rattling in the next room. A painfully fat man sat at a desk shuffling papers looking busy, official. No one seemed very interested in our wedding, not even the Justice of the Peace, who looked rather irritated by his job of marriage. Did he know something I didn't?

The ceremony took about ten minutes. Standing next to Ben with Sam and Bobby on either side of us, I suddenly wished my mother was there. I wanted my mother. It surprised me because I had told her we would get married in Boston because Ben had business there—a small lie to keep her away. Thinking about it now made my eyelids sting.

When it was time to say goodbye to her that afternoon, I had to lean over in my new high heels to hug her small frame. I held my mother lightly and gravely. It made me feel as if I was the mother. "Take care of yourself, Mama," I said, "I'll send you some money as soon as I can." My mother clung to my neck for a moment and then looked at me sadly. Maybe she'll get a boyfriend when I've gone, I thought, knowing the idea was silly. Maybe a Synagogue elder. Or the old widower who moved in on the first floor. I wished someone, anyone, would remove the burden I felt as I leaned over again to hug my mother's fragile bones. I turned away from her wet-eyed mournful gaze and struggled once again with my familiar, bewildering guilt for the bunions on my mother's feet and her loneliness and my unworthy absent father; for following his abandonment with my own. I wanted to go back to my tight little room, unpack my valise, and sit on my bed. But I fought it off. I would not stay with my mother. I was going to get married.

So I picked up my new valise and new beige purse and left the apartment, closing the door softly behind me. Standing there in the hall smelling its peculiar mixture of cabbage and grief, my heart pounding, I opened the door for a last look at my mother. She was praying with her eyes closed. Every time she turned from gin to God (my two G's she would say when she was in a good mood) it was a familiar sight to me. She would pray on her knees twice daily, a practice she had adopted from her Catholic husband, the first thing in the morning and when she came home from work still smelling of permanent wave chemicals. Then for hours afterward she looked distracted and sly as if she were deep in private conversation with herself.

I closed the door quietly again, hoping my mother was praying for me. I was scared. But when I hurried to the streetcar stop in my high-heeled tottering little steps, wearing the beige mink-trimmed suit that Ben bought me to be married in, my valise banging against my knee, I felt a guilty and powerful tremble of freedom, as if I could hear the jail door clang shut behind me, as if I were free, as if right here, right now, instead of passing the Quik Fix Shoe Repair on the sidewalk I could soar like a bird, valise and all, right over the A & P and Woolworth's and Allen's Drug Store. My heart was making a great commotion in my chest. I would not have to see my mother mutter to herself. Or the dusty, damp shadowy apartment with its smell of the sauerkraut she took to eating in large quantities every time she stopped drinking. Or my hot little room or my mother's desperate piety. I would not have to wait without hope for my father's return. I had cut myself loose, my freedom made more daring, more audacious, by the delicate thrill I felt marrying a man I had known only a few months. It was breathtaking.

When the streetcar came I struggled up the steps in my narrow skirt and settled myself on the cane bench, my valise nudging my foot. It is true that I rode to my wedding alone on a streetcar, but my vision of deliverance was such that the strangers scattered on the cane seats could have been my parents and bridesmaids riding along with me in a big gleaming Packard.

* * *

After the ceremony, our wedding party walked the short distance from the City Hall to the hotel. I hobbled along in my first high heels with Ben carrying my valise, politely holding my elbow up and down the curbs. Just ahead, Sam and Bobby walked in unison like miscast bridesmaids, turning around every few minutes to wait for Ben and me to catch up. Sam moved in that light, easy, graceful way of boxers and Bobby walked sort of pigeon-toed, like a boy. As we walked, I noticed Sam remove his yarmulke and stuff it in his pocket.

In the Hollendon, the best hotel in town, tall gilded pillars and an elaborate ceiling of golden leaves and cupids framed shabby furniture and carpet gone threadbare—then a familiar sight in hotel lobbies all over the country. Four or five apparently jobless men sat around on the cracked leather chairs with their fedoras on, reading newspapers or smoking, with vacant eyes. One was asleep with his mouth open. A couple of the men looked up over their newspapers as the four of us passed in our wedding finery, but the lobby was so quiet I could hear my dress brush against my silk stockings. We rode up in the elevator and followed Bobby to a door at the end of the corridor marked "Embassy Suite." The room had large dirty windows and stiff gilt chairs. A round table was in the center with silver candlesticks bordering a bouquet of white roses and trays of fancy little canapés.

* * *

When the door was closed Sam went into the bathroom and came out with a bottle of champagne. After he filled the glasses all around with his small hairy hands, he raised his, and said, "Mazl Tov! To my boss and the prettiest bride I've ever seen." He was tall and thickly built with dark skin and nervous brown eyes. His hair was black and combed straight back without a part.

Ben looked happy, his eyes the color of sand, Sam's dark face was moist with perspiration, and Bobby, leaning against the wall, sipping champagne, knowing the right things to say, reminded me of that slender man posed in the cigarette ad in *Vanity Fair* with a beautiful blonde woman on his arm. We stood around holding canapés. Sam munched his with a little finger sticking up in the air while Ben went back and forth to the bathroom for more champagne. No one sat on the small gilt chairs. I looked from one to the other, thinking what an odd little wedding, as if it was happening to someone else. I hadn't expected to feel like this, like Alice, as if I had been transported into a strange land of unlikely people. For a moment I felt as if I was actually shrinking. I held myself up and concentrated on being in love with Ben, with his grand style, his thrilling power, his splendid smile. After a while Bobby put his glass down, shook hands with Ben, kissed me on the cheek, and left the room, taking Sam with him.

We spent our wedding night in the bridal suite. Ben swung open the door; there were huge vases of white, long-stemmed roses everywhere—on the end tables, the coffee table, the bureaus—even on the floor. They smelled oppressive to me, excessive and ominous, the aroma of grand funerals. On the big turned-back bed a white satin nightgown was spread out that looked to me like the gown of

Aphrodite as she sprang from the foam of the sea. Music drifted through the rooms from a radio somewhere as Ben popped open more champagne and poured it, pale and shimmering, into our glasses. We toasted our future and sipped. Then, as if silently cued from backstage, a waiter wheeled in a cart bearing silver-domed plates of foods I had never seen before. For years I could not hear certain songs or taste certain foods without the same mix of excitement and unaccountable uneasiness that I felt that night for my hours-old marriage. "The Man I Love," the radio sang, as I dipped the delicate poached salmon, pink and cold, into the queer-tasting caviar sauce. Afterwards, "My Melancholy Baby" always made me think of the moist, tender squab and firm gray-brown granules of gamey wild rice tucked inside. Dessert was Peach Melba served in high-stemmed goblets. We ate and sipped champagne and I felt each strange new taste and texture on my tongue, in my nose, my mouth, as it passed my throat. We spoke little, as if words had no place in such rooms sensuous with exotic flavors, love songs, the thick scent of roses, and a gown on the bed for a love goddess. Ben kept my glass filled with champagne and between courses pulled me to my feet to dance, holding me close, humming off-key in my ear.

Later, I was as nervous and ignorant as any eighteen-year-old virgin in spite of all the reading I had done—including what was then called a *Marriage Manual* that spoke of simultaneous orgasms and had alarming illustrations of the erect male organ. That night in the big bed my passion abandoned me and I couldn't figure out what all the fuss was about—why Anna Karenina gave up her son, her country, and even her life, or why Emma Bovary allowed her obsessions to cause her own ruin and death. But the problem wasn't Ben's lovemaking. The truth is that my father's Catholicism I thought I left behind, had returned, unbidden, to find myself still unmarried in the eyes of the church. And although I had long since given up both my mother's Judaism and my father's Catholicism, there were times that I believed the events that followed were my punishment for the sin of fornication.

* * *

After a honeymoon in Manhattan, I settled into Ben's house. The upstairs was as luxurious as the living room; each bedroom had thick white carpeting, carved bureaus, entire walls of mirrors, silk-cushioned chaise lounges, swags and swags of white silk draperies. And a bathroom all to myself that was huge and had steaming water that poured from the mouths of golden swans perched on a marble tub bigger than my bed at home. Ben's closet held more clothes than I had ever seen in one place, as many, I was sure, as the men's section of

Halle's Department Store. His suits were neatly arranged by color and season, the dark blues and grays giving way along the rack to the summer creams and whites. Shallow drawers held rows of jeweled cuff links, a rainbow of ties stretched along a wall, and dozens of stiff-collared silk shirts hung neatly in whites and pastels. Ben caught me in there, touching and staring. He laughed at me and took me to bed. (The shotgun I later saw standing in the corner wasn't there then, or did I refuse to believe my own eyes?)

Since my small valise had been filled with more journals than clothes, (keeping journals had been my passion from the time I was ten years old) on our wedding trip Ben outfitted me from the skin out at Bergdorf Goodman, while outside William Randolph Hearst's truck doled out soup to people in a line so long it snaked down Fifth Avenue for six blocks. Trailing an entourage of fawning salespeople and floor managers, Ben felt the silk, blew at the fur, studied the match of the purse's alligator skins, took the hat to the window light, and sent me, blushing, to try on a white marabou-trimmed negligee and nightgown.

We had arrived at Bergdorf's after a lunch at the Stork Club of beef tenderloin with a sauce of mushrooms, tiny browned potatoes, asparagus spears, and scarlet aspic. Afterwards, walking along Fifth Avenue, warmed by the good scotch I had sipped and the winter sun on my back, I felt a languor deep in my flesh, a sensual, fleshy pleasure totally unlike my old gratification of books and study. But those days were over. And good riddance. Don't you think I knew I could have been standing in that soup line we passed?

From the moment I walked into the department store on Ben's arm (recognizing the perfumed air as the singular smell of the rich), I felt as if I had drifted into a fantasy. But it was a real saleswoman who came into the fitting room bringing me tea in a china cup, and then the clothes Ben selected for me to try on; silken daytime ensembles in jeweled colors, wool suits trimmed in fox and beaver. Flirtatiously brimmed and veiled hats. Alone in the mirrored dressing room, I strutted and posed in my new clothes. I couldn't help it. I felt suddenly endowed with exemplary character, different in my skin, as transformed as the drab smelly gym on prom night.

See Vivian? I wanted to say, you were dead wrong. Look at me now.

We came home with a wardrobe for a princess and Ben went back to work, joining Bobby and Sam in the basement offices. After I glimpsed its wood paneling once or twice, the office doors stayed firmly shut and I got the unmistakable message that I would not be welcome down there. Bobby and Sam were always around—Bobby in his office, Sam sitting in the basement reception room when he wasn't driving Ben or Bobby somewhere in the big black Packard sedan.

Bobby and Sam came and went through the basement entrance that opened off the driveway; each had a key. Sam's green Pontiac coupe, Bobby's silver Pierce Arrow, and the black Packard were parked in the driveway in that order, never on the street, even though there was often an inconvenient shuffling of cars in and out of the driveway. Bobby always left the house at five, but Sam was never farther away than the basement reception room, except when he went home to sleep. Ben told me that Sam was thirty-six, but with his girth and tight suits and aloof, nervous eyes he seemed older to me.

Every month or so the four of us drove to New York in the big Packard with Sam behind the wheel, Bobby in the front passenger seat, and Ben and me in the back; a journey of two days over mountains and narrow, winding roads, some unpaved. When we arrived we would check into our suite at the Plaza with our fourteen pieces of luggage, and go out on the town.

One night as we were dressing, the phone rang.

I picked it up. "Hello?"

"Is Benny there?"

"It's for you," I said, handing him the phone.

"See who it is," he said, frowning.

"Who is calling?" I asked into the phone.

"Goddamn it, tell him it's his mother. Tell him I'm downstairs."

"It's your mother," I said. "She's downstairs."

"Hang up," Ben said.

Back then I didn't think Ben could surprise me. I hung up the phone.

It rang again. This time a man's voice. "Mrs. Bernstein to see Mr. Gold."

I covered the mouthpiece and turned to Ben. "Mrs. Bernstein wants to see you."

"Say I'm in a meeting," Ben said.

"He's in a meeting," I said into the phone and hung up.

"My mother lives in New York," Ben said, "and calls the Plaza constantly to see if I'm here so she can drive me crazy."

"Your mother? But her name's Bernstein."

In the corridor a luggage cart rumbled by. Outside, a siren howled.

"Husband number three or four. I lost count."

There was a sudden pounding on the door. I got up and opened it. Ben stood stone-faced.

A woman rushed past me. Her piled-up hair was dyed a doll's yellow, her thin lips and bony cheeks painted a clown's red. Somehow, the overall effect was that of an overweight, fixed-up corpse.

Ben sat down wearily on the bed. "Mama, I'm busy."

"Benny! I had to give the schmuck twenty bucks to get the room number!" she cried. She wore a long, flowered dress and thick black shoes that laced up the ankle. She reeked of drugstore perfume. Lilac.

She turned to me. "Who's this?"

"My wife, Kate."

"Is she Jewish? She doesn't look Jewish."

"Mama," Ben said, getting up, taking her elbow firmly and walking her to the door. "I'm busy now," he said again. "Go on home. I'll call you."

"No, you won't, you never call me! Benny never calls me!" she shouted to me over Ben's shoulder.

Ben had finally maneuvered her to the door when she suddenly shook her arm free. "Don't push me!"

"Okay. Just leave. Please."

"Mister big deal! Mister hot shot! Mister rich man doesn't want to see his own mother!" She announced to the room. "Mister big shot pushes his own mother!"

"Okay, Mama, okay," Ben said. And Mrs. Bernstein found herself outside in the hall with the door shut firmly behind her.

"Benny! You damn Mr. Bitch!" Mrs. Bernstein screamed over several loud thuds on the door, as if being kicked by one of those laced-up shoes.

Ben turned to the mirror, tied his black tie and put on his tuxedo jacket, as if his crazy mother hadn't just revealed herself to me, as if she didn't exist. I started to speak, but he turned to me with such hostile eyes I was stopped cold. His mother was off limits, along with the basement office and his nightly disappearances.

"Get dressed, Kate," he said. "We're late."

I slipped into a bronze V-necked chiffon gown that hung in points from a band of golden beads at the hip, and as we were about to leave for the Stork Club, Ben surprised me with a white fox coat and diamond earrings. When Bobby saw me he threw himself on the floor pretending to collapse at the sight of my splendor.

Even years later I remembered the moment we entered the speakeasy that night—I see my young self as if I were looking at a snapshot: the four of us are poised in tableau; I am second from the left, standing there with flaming hair, glittering ears, that absurd white fox coat to my ankles, and ample cleavage. Ben is smiling on my left, looking smart and sly as if he owns the place, Bobby and Sam are on my right—Bobby next to me, relaxed, elegant, his hands in his pockets, Sam a little apart, looking wary. The band is playing "Sweet Georgia Brown" as Sherman Billingsley welcomes us in his Oklahoma drawl, hugging Ben, kissing me on the cheek, shaking hands with Bobby and Sam. He leads me to our ringside table, my peculiar little family following in single file as we move through the crowded, dim room (Ben, then Bobby, then Sam lumbering along the rear), hearing the sweet jazzy sounds of the trumpets and clarinets, feeling the pounding of the piano and drums vibrating the floor under my feet, feeling the stares and whispers as we pass, feeling beautiful and rich and safe, feeling the moment powerfully as if it would last forever, the princess in the fairy tale living on after the last page. I was eighteen years old and thought Ben Gold had taken me straight up to heaven with one stop along the way at Bergdorf Goodman's to dress for the ride. I thought I had brought it off. I thought I had rescued myself. I really did. I could not bring myself to believe that everything I was feeling was not love. Or that this extravagant luxury was not happiness. Or that Ben's moods and nightly disappearances were anything other than his preoccupation with important business affairs.

We dined elegantly on those trips at Owney Madden's Club Napoleon with its revolving bar and three floors of velvet and mirrors. One night at El Morocco, Lucky Luciano greeted Ben with a big bear hug and insisted on taking us to his speakeasy, The House Of Morgan. After listening to Helen Morgan sing "My Man" as she sat on the piano, the five of us made the rounds to Legs Diamonds' Hotsy Totsy, and the Embassy Club, then owned by Dutch Schultz. We drank only champagne; we listened to wonderful jazz—Jimmy McPartland, Bix Beiderbecke, Eddie Condon, Art Tatum. And we never went to New York without going downstairs at the Park Central Hotel to hear Bessie Smith sing "St. Louis Blues" in her powerful, heartbreaking voice.

We went to the theater. "The Barretts of Wimpole Street;" Noel Coward's "Private Lives." "The Zigfield Follies of 1931," whose long-legged beauties made me think painfully of Vivian.

When the weather was good for the journey home, Bobby brought along a picnic from the Stork Club. Sam would stop the big Packard about two o'clock and Bobby would set up the folding table and chairs in a secluded, wooded spot. After we were seated, Bobby always whipped out a tablecloth and napkins like a blond matador, and with great flourishes served succulent capons; there'd be plum soup, chilled and tart, or a velvety pate—once we had mushrooms stuffed with Roquefort. Our favorite dessert was a Stork Club specialty; bananas baked to a golden bronze and served in a dark syrupy sauce. Ben poured the champagne that Sherman Billingsley had packed in ice. Back in the car I would fall asleep with my head on Ben's shoulder until we arrived at the Hotel Harrisburg, our overnight stop.

* * *

But as the months passed the luxuries in my life seemed to lose their fascination. When I asked Ben about his strange hours and mysterious comings and goings, he said, "Listen, in these times I have to hustle business wherever I can find it." Questioning him another time he told me he had a few lonely customers who insisted on doing business at night. After that he angrily accused me of not trusting him and said the subject was closed.

So I backed off with not a little relief. There was something in the air I did not want to know. It made me tired. It exhausted me. I discovered that not knowing was hard work. A kind of paralysis of my will set in as if I had abandoned my volition for Ben's. I did as I was told. I tried to please. We went out most nights, usually to Allie's, the best speakeasy in town. I dressed carefully for those evenings, as if gowns cut low in shimmering fabrics that closely followed my body could convince me of my place on Ben's arm and in his life.

Chapter 6

A laundress came twice a week, and Francine, who had been Ben's housekeeper for years, did the cleaning and cooking. I liked Francine— her wholesome, church-going presence reassured me. She seemed kind and motherly and I hung around her chattering like a schoolgirl, hoping for some maternal wisdom for the confused dislocation I felt. But after Francine courteously declined several invitations to sit down with me for a cup of coffee, I wondered if she resented her boss's dressed-up bride. Or if maybe Francine thought I was trying to pry Ben's secrets from her. Or that she was worried I could fire her. I began to feel as if I had been transported from my simple, unwanted world that was everything it seemed, to a slippery Byzantine mansion of surfaces and secrets. I slept late. I read stories by Collette. I wrote in my journal. I took my time getting dressed in my beautiful new clothes. I went to the beauty shop. Not Irene's, where my mother worked, but Jacques, downtown.

Early for my appointment one Friday, I waited in the reception room watching the slim young women and fashionable matrons getting their hair set. At Irene's, the ladies were older, with thinning gray hair that barely covered pink scalps, plump middle-aged women in lisle stockings and sensible shoes. Even the magazines were different; Jacques' had shiny new copies of *Vogue* and *Good Housekeeping*; at Irene's, there were two-year-old piles of dog-eared issues of *True Confessions* and *Hollywood Stars*. Jacques' shop was painted a gleaming pink with chairs the exact same color; the floor was covered in shining, bold pink and white squares. All the beauty operators wore pink uniforms that were repeated into infinity in the walls of sparkling mirrors. My mother had two uniforms, one blue and the other maroon, which she alternated wearing, washing and ironing them every other night. With its peeling beige walls and fading cracked linoleum, Irene's shop had always seemed sort of seedy to me; now it brought tears to my eyes. Sitting in Jacques' gleaming pink reception room, I felt more displaced than ever, disloyal to my mother, a traitor.

Every day, from fourth grade until Windsor Danbury, I had sat in the back of Irene's Beauty Shop under a broken hair dryer doing my homework. The shop became my second home; a feminine world of heavy sweet smells and rattling bottles, soft skin and fleshy shapes. There were no class distinctions while hair was being waved and bobby-pinned with sticky setting-lotion; in that place, at that moment, there was only one universe: that of being a woman. I soon understood the shorthand of the closed-in sisterhood of secret, small-spaced wisdom; a peculiarly feminine wisdom, without grandeur or ambition, kept hidden and used only as needed. There would be a certain look in the eye, a raised eyebrow, a knowing laugh, a nod of appreciation in an unspoken conspiracy of rapport and refuge from the irrational demands and consequences of the male world. Then, hair freshly shampooed and set, they would go home to their insecure, demanding men whom they carefully protected and nurtured, well taught by their mothers.

I did not want any of those female stories I overheard of wash days and men to wait on; men they seemed to fear and ridicule, need and reject; men they mocked, rolling their eyes. I did not want their resentment or their days of numbing, thankless chores or their emotional isolation or the drink that made it bearable. Sitting under the broken hair dryer, I knew this only dimly, but the insight had a firefly's stubborn, intermittent glow. There was, it seemed, men's work and women's work; men's lives and women's lives. I knew what to choose. I was going to be a writer. Wasn't I already writing in my journal every day? Stories. Profiles of my teachers and friends. Accounts of my daily activities. My secret feelings. Nature. Animals. Landscapes and details of my small world. Writing was the best part of my day and I always saved it for last—like dessert—after school and homework and Mrs. Shapiro and chores.

At first, of course, the very idea of becoming an author was too absurd for a child of poverty, born of a drinking mother and runaway father, and even after I got the scholarship to Windsor Danbury I didn't tell anyone except Vivian. But as time went on I stopped being intimidated by my audacity. I had won a scholarship to the academically-respected Windsor Danbury, hadn't I? I was smart. I loved English; I loved writing. Freud said anatomy was destiny, but I would move as far away from my fate as the moon. I would write books.

"Step this way, Mrs. Gold," said the unsmiling, beautiful receptionist. "Jacques is ready for you."

"No, no thank you," I said, to my surprise. "I'm going to see my mother," I added politely.

"I beg your pardon?"

But I was already on my way.

* * *

When I saw my mother setting her customer's hair in her oversized shoes, I felt such a rush of love and memory that my eyes moistened. Irene was working to my mother's left, Mattie to her right, Lena, who only worked Fridays and Saturdays, at the end of the row, in the same hierarchy of positions they had had for years. My mother's chair was next to Irene's, which always gave me a twinge of pride. Even drinking and often late or absent, the number-two chair was hers in spite of Mattie's and Lena's objections. But my mother's customers always returned when Irene called and told them Annie Brady was back. Besides, by that time my father's checks had completely stopped and Irene was not an unsympathetic woman.

Sitting in Jacques' pink and white salon I had felt such cruel nostalgia for that place, for my mother, that I had to remind myself I couldn't wait to leave, that I had married a stranger to get away. Now, watching my mother in this familiar, gentle place, I felt like myself again, real again, rooted somewhere I understood. I looked out the plate glass window to my old neighborhood—the A & P, the streetcar stop at Allen's Drug Store where Mr. Allen always made Vivian and me special cokes with extra cherry syrup, while outside, the streets came alive as the public school let out. Across the street stood Woolworth's, reminding me of its September-smell of notebooks, pencils, rulers, paste, and the excitement and dread of going back to school. Just out of sight were the side-streets of Webster and Clifford with their ancient leafy trees and decaying houses where the spinsters and retired couples lived, and two blocks away, over near the elementary school, on Rodale and Findley, kids chased by yapping dogs played on small lawns, spilling into the streets.

I watched my mother work on her customer. Her hands were skillful and steady as she made finger waves and twirled locks of hair, anchoring them down with bobby pins. This was my mother of the outside world, normal and competent. It did not surprise me; I well knew that there were two mothers. At work or Synagogue her hands never trembled; she was cheerful and capable—at home with me she seemed shaken and bewildered, as if only the surprises and anarchy of the outside world required her equilibrium. I did not know how she managed these transformations. I couldn't even tell which was my real mother. Standing there, watching, I had a simple, swift wish—that I had a different mother, the kind whose husband didn't run out on her. Who would be sitting next to my father in a Studebaker, come to take me home because I called them up and said I was worried sick about my husband's nightly disappearances.

"It's Katie!" Irene cried, and six heads jerked toward me in unison. My mother dropped her comb on the counter and rushed toward me, arms outstretched. I felt her familiar bony contours as we hugged, (my mother still did not eat properly) smelling her familiar scent of wave-set lotion and sauerkraut. Lena, shampooing a customer, was smiling at me, up to her wrists in soap. Now Irene was hugging me, and then Mattie, both women unchanged since I was a child; Mattie looking as copper-haired and plump, her bosom straining the buttons of her uniform, and Irene as wrinkled and solid. (In her own estimation, Irene was one of the fortunate few. She worked in her shop, she worked in her garden, she could recite Edgar Guest, she cheerfully appreciated that—as she often said—the beauty shop business was depression-proof, her ladies always managing her fifty cents for a shampoo and set.)

Mattie, Irene, and Annie were all talking at once, admiring me, fingering my mauve wool suit with its beaver collar. Then Mattie yanked at her girdle and hurried back to her customer.

"Annie, you go on with Katie," Irene said. "I'll put Mrs. Backus under the dryer."

"Let's go over to Feldman's," my mother said, smiling with her outside face. "Have you had lunch?"

We walked around the corner together, mother and daughter, to Feldman's Delicatessen. Inside, I breathed the nostalgic smell of pastrami and pickles. It was late for lunch, and the place was almost empty. As we sat in one of the booths my mother called to Arnold, who was reading a newspaper behind the counter, to bring us two cups of coffee and two corned beef sandwiches. Then she leaned back in the booth, inhaled deeply and closed her eyes. When she looked at me again, her eyes were wet.

"Months go by and I don't see you," she said. "I don't even know where you live."

"I live at fourteen ninety-six Chatterton. You know that."

"So what? I have no idea where that is."

"Mama, I've called you seven, eight times. At least."

"Called. The telephone. And always at the shop when I'm too busy to talk."

"I can't very well call you at home when you don't have a phone."

She gazed at me for a long moment. Then she said, "That's right. Blame it on me."

I felt myself grow heavy all the way down to my feet. "Mama, I'm not blaming you," I said. It was the truth. Even then I knew not to blame her. But at some level I tried to avoid, I did. I blamed her. "Please,

Mama. Let's have a nice visit."

My mother reached into her pocket and withdrew a handkerchief with shaking hands.

I opened my purse and handed her an envelope.

She opened it and flushed a deep red. "Fifty dollars!" she cried, looking up and smiling. "Well! Well, thanks. Thank you."

"I'm late, I have to go," I said.

"But you haven't had lunch—"

"I'll tell Arnold and get the check," I said, getting up. I leaned over and kissed my mother's cool, rubbery cheek. "'Bye, Mama. I'll call you soon."

I had not meant to rush away like that without making the connection I had imagined. (Well! My mother would say, with a big happy smile. How are you, Katie honey? How's married life? What a gorgeous wedding ring! How about you two coming over Friday night for a good meal? Ben's colored maid cook's goyisha food, and I'll make him matzo ball soup, brisket, noodle kugel. I'll make him a nice sponge cake.)

But I knew it would be just like it was. I always knew.

* * *

A week or so later, after another one of those midnight telephone calls that took Ben out into the night, I lay there watching the clock, so furious at Ben, at myself, at my stoic apathy and willful ignorance, that I suddenly got up, went into the closet to pack and stared at the shotgun standing in the corner, this time actually seeing it. I packed a valise and took it downstairs. As I put it into the front closet I felt an immense rush of relief, as if I were reclaiming something that belonged to me. I went back upstairs and fell into such a sound sleep I didn't hear Ben come home and get into bed.

When I came downstairs the next morning Ben was at the breakfast table reading the newspaper. I sat down. He said good morning and went back to his paper.

I decided to give him one more chance before I left. I didn't know why. So I said, where were you last night? He said something vague, like 'out', or 'I had to go downtown.' Then he said, well, aren't you the curious one. So I asked him again, loudly, probably too loudly, because he jerked up from his newspaper so violently he knocked over the coffee Francine had put in front of me.

"Enough. That's enough. No more questions," he said, with his icy yellow gaze. "I don't talk business." He went back to his paper while Francine silently wiped up the coffee and poured another cup for me from the big percolator in the kitchen.

I got up from the table, went to the telephone, and called a taxi.

He looked up. "Where do you think you're going?"

I took my coat and valise out of the closet. "I'll send for the rest of my things," I said, heading for the window to watch for the cab.

I heard him get up from the table and come over to me. I felt his breath on my neck.

"I'm sorry, Kate."

I didn't move.

"I'm sorry," he said again, to my back. "It's just that, you know, I hate burdening you with my business problems. I was with a customer with a drinking problem—he's the guy who always calls me and I can't turn him down because he gives me so much business." He put his hands on my shoulders and turned me toward him. "Forgive me, Kate," he said softly. "I was wrong. I shouldn't have spoken to you like that."

"The shotgun," I said, backing up, "in the closet."

He dropped his hands and shrugged. "Protection. This crazy client loses his watch, I tell him it isn't covered so he goes bananas on me and starts threatening." He shook his head sadly. "Kate, you have to understand, these are tough times—my God, people going crazy, jumping out of windows; you read about it every day. I assure you I'm not taking any chances with some poor bastard going off his rocker."

He picked up the valise at my feet, took my hand, and led me upstairs. I let him. Inside the bedroom he closed the door. Then he opened my valise and dumped my clothes out on the bed while I stood watching. He turned to me, unbuttoned my dress and slipped it off. He took off my bra. He unhooked my stockings and peeled them off, then he unfastened my garter belt and slid off my panties, kissing my body along the way. I let him. I was excited. When I was naked, he unbuttoned his trousers and we made love on the floor.

My own actions were as unaccountable to me as his hidden life. Yes, I wanted to believe his story. And okay, he excited me. But I had already discovered that Hemingway left out the part about the earth waiting there as solid and troubled as before it started moving under you. So did I stay because it was unthinkable to return to my mother? Or because I couldn't get my hands on any money? (Francine did the food shopping and Ben insisted that I charge what I wanted.) Or was I afraid of Ben's shrouded life? Or fascinated by it? Or was I simply a coward, corrupted by my life of luxury? I did not know. Feeling too confused, too helplessly stuck, and too far gone in my unexpected and unwanted life, that night I couldn't even write in my journal.

* * *

The next morning a note of congratulations arrived from Vivian, addressed to "Mr. & Mrs. Benjamin Gold." Although its late arrival and formality stung, I was relieved that at least she hadn't completely ignored the wedding announcement I had sent her months ago. I wrote an equally brief note, thanking her. Vivian responded a month later, still stiffly. I didn't know how to break through her icy formality, or even if I wanted to. I didn't know if I was angry with Vivian for being right, or at myself for being stubborn and stupid. So when I finally did write, I did not tell her that Ben's basement offices were off limits to me, as well as the truth. Or about his moods that could change from charm to icy fury in a confusing, frightening moment—or how his shouts of anger bewildered and scared me, erupting over anything from overcooked eggs to whatever it was that took place behind his closed office doors.

And I didn't tell her about Bobby. About how I watched for him from my window every morning, and how merely his blond, lean presence seemed to make me short of breath. Or that every time he declined Ben's invitation to come with us to Allie's I was stunned with disappointment—and when he did come, how I had to concentrate on not looking at him. Filled with self-contempt, Vivian was the last person in the world I wanted to know about the submissive, confused woman I had become.

So I answered her note in defiance, pride, and misery, writing as if I were the same ambitious, independent person with audacious goals that Vivian knew. I told her about our glamorous trips to New York. I told her what I wore to Owney Madden's Club Napoleon. I wrote about our champagne picnics, describing the weather and food, the flora and fauna. Then I made stuff up about Ben's kindness, his loving attention, and his thriving insurance business—a fiction worthy of an A in Windsor Danbury's senior creative writing class.

Chapter 7

After I missed a second period, I went to the doctor. In the examination room I was handed a smock and told to strip from the waist down except for my shoes. (The shoes part puzzled me, but I followed orders and soon learned they were a necessary part of the humiliation that was to follow.) The heels of my shoes in stirrups, eyes glued to the ceiling, the doctor's head disappeared between my pushed-apart knees, I was told to relax (relax!) while feeling his rubber-gloved hand painfully probing deeply hidden organs I didn't know I had. He finally removed the hand that felt like a fist, pulled off the rubber glove and told me what I had already figured out. I was stunned anyway. Even then I wrote in my book that I knew I was finished with something. With being young.

Arriving as it did, a few days later, Vivian's affectionate letter of apology felt strangely anti-climatic to me, irrelevant almost, its timing as off as that of my marriage, my coming motherhood, my bewildering life. I wrote her about the baby. Vivian responded warmly, and although we began corresponding, I was too embarrassed over my lies to tell the truth now. Besides, I knew all Vivian could do was give me glib advice, and I felt another cruel stab of envy at the opposite direction our lives had taken.

Ben was thrilled, but all I could feel was trapped. And confused. One moment I was tormented with regret, the next fantasizing how this baby would somehow fix everything. After all, I told myself, it was always Ben who peered under the hood of a baby carriage on the street, smiling, asking the baby's name, making silly cooing and clicking noises until I pulled him away. And when Sam's sister brought her four year old over for Sunday dinner that time, it was Ben who got down on the floor and played with the child for an hour with the dolls and crayons he kept in a box for the little girl. Yes. It was not impossible that a baby would change our marriage. It has been known to happen.

He lavished me with attention. Well, not exactly attention; it was more as if I were made of glass or suffering from a terminal disease. Unasked, he'd dash upstairs for my sweater. Mornings he brought hot tea to me in bed (forbidding the coffee I loved) and warm milk in the evenings before he went out. Then I'd wake up in a sweat from the extra blankets he piled on top of me when he came home. He even pored over the book on pregnancy I got from the library. It had a chapter on the death of newborns that I skipped because it scared me. But Ben read the book from cover to cover on Sundays after dinner, before playing his operas on the Victrola. When we walked he held my elbow in an iron grip as if my legs were made of water. He constantly asked me how I felt, if I was warm enough, was I tired, did I want anything, was I getting enough fresh air, exercise, sleep. He drove me crazy. Especially when he did his usual table-hopping at Allie's and told everyone I was pregnant while I sat with Sam at our table, blushing.

All I thought about was food. I sneaked downstairs in the middle of the night and ate peanut butter out of the jar with my finger. Eating breakfast, I plotted lunch. At dinner, while Francine and Ben stared, I had second and third helpings of everything Francine put in front of me. Even the carrots I had loathed. And bread. I couldn't seem to get enough bread.

* * *

"Hi, Red," Bobby said.

"Hello, Bobby."

He plopped down on the yellow velvet couch and put his feet up. "What're you writing?"

I had been working on my book, writing a scene about the fight I had with Vivian when she told me not to marry Ben because his friend got those scabs beaten up and two of them killed.

"Taking notes," I lied. My book was my secret. So I held up the copy of *Daisy Miller* at my side.

"My old friend, *Daisy Miller*. Haven't seen her since college."

"What are you doing upstairs in the middle of the day?" I asked him.

"Came to pry you away from that book. We're going for a walk."

I put the book down. "A walk? At two o'clock in the afternoon? *You*?"

"Why not? Little mothers need fresh air and exercise."

For an instant I caught myself in a sweet fantasy that Bobby was my baby's father. But something was going on that brought me back to earth fast; what could bring Bobby upstairs to me at two o'clock in the afternoon?

"Come on, Bobby," I said. "You haven't taken a walk in the middle of the afternoon in your life."

"Well, well, isn't the redhead suspicious."

"You're damn right."

"I'm playing hooky," Bobby said, grinning.

"With all those girlfriends you're playing hooky to walk with me?"

"Sure," he said, cheerfully.

"People don't play hooky to walk with pregnant ladies."

"Especially when they're pregnant by someone else." He looked at me. "Red, you blush faster and redder than any man or woman I ever did see. Is that why your name's Red?"

I didn't want his banter. I wanted to ask him what really went on down in that basement. But I didn't. Maybe I was afraid he'd tell me. Then what would I do? I said nothing and turned back to *Daisy Miller*.

"No more reading, little mother. On your feet. You're going for a walk," he said, standing up.

I looked at him. "Not until you tell me why you're up here."

He opened his mouth and closed it again.

"Come on, Bobby, come clean."

He paused again. "I'm assigned."

"You're what?"

He put his hands in his pockets and looked up at the ceiling. "Wrong word. Sorry."

"Bobby, what's going on?"

"Ben sent me to keep you company," he said, still not looking at me.

Was this some kind of diabolical test Ben devised to trap me? Did I talk in my sleep or something? Has he noticed the way my traitorous face turns red whenever Bobby's around?

"I'm supposed to help you pass the time," Bobby said.

Of course. Now I understood. For the last three or four months Ben had begun taking my pregnancy for granted, stopping his attentions, slipping back into his old habits. Which should not have surprised or disappointed me. But it did, and after all that lavished attention I felt lonelier than ever, often finding myself in tears over nothing and frequently, unaccountably furious—when the alarm clock rang I wanted to fling it across the room. Once I did. And immensely enjoyed the shocked look on Ben's face when it crashed through the window. Yesterday at breakfast I started to talk to him about something and when he merely grunted, I grabbed the newspaper out of his hand. My bravery came from the protection I knew I had from his unborn child whom he already loved beyond all else. So although his eyes turned to yellow ice and his face colored, he merely got up and stamped down to the basement office.

And just last night, trying to sleep on my back—the only position now available to me—my head throbbed, my back ached, and I felt little rivers of sweat run between my breasts down to my belly where they were stopped by that small mountain. Ben finally came home after three, which was not unusual, fouling the air with the same whisky stench as my mother's, which was also not unusual. But this time I was wide awake. And furious. When he slipped into bed I sat up and exploded. Tears and complaints flowed out of me like blood from a wound. Ben got out of bed and went into the bathroom. I shrieked to the closed door of my loneliness and isolation. I hollered to the bedside lamp about his secretiveness and life apart. I wailed to the thin air about his mysterious disappearances. He didn't come out of the bathroom until I had exhausted myself and collapsed back on the pillow with a pounding heart.

Now comes Bobby, ordered to keep me occupied, keep me quiet, keep me away. Well, at least it was an improvement over the bathroom door and the back Ben turned to me when he got back into bed. I wondered, embarrassed, if he had told Bobby about the scenes I'd been making.

"What did Ben say?" I asked him.

"I told you. He said to keep you company." He looked at me. "Don't be upset, Red, he means well."

Well, in my present condition—as they called it in those days—I certainly wanted to believe that he meant well. One morning, early in my pregnancy, when our lovemaking had gone beyond Ben's fierce solitary passion, I felt something almost sweet in him, a kind of tenderness, and a response of looseness and ease in my own body that kept my heart pounding and body pulsing long after the rush of desire and heat. Ben reached for my hand after that; he smelled slightly sweaty, musky, thick; it was an intimate scent not related to his closed face and crisp, remote daytime presence and violently changing moods. His eyes were a soft amber in the morning light, and even his hands seemed softer than they did in his perfectly cut suits. (Ben always wore a shirt, tie and suit even downstairs to the basement office, while Bobby, only a few years younger, looked like his son, or the college boyfriend of my fantasies, in his sweater and pale, wide-legged trousers). After a while, after being quiet, still holding my hand, Ben began to talk. He told me how his father went from job to job, selling junk from a pushcart, working in a cigar factory, on a Ford assembly line, a garment factory, a restaurant. He said he bought back the samovar his father had had to sell, but that he didn't live to see it. He spoke without looking at me, but I thought I saw his eyes glisten. Feeling a wave of tenderness, I moved toward him. But he turned away and hurried out of bed.

"Come on, Red, a deal's a deal," Bobby was saying. "You made me tell and you're going for a walk."

I looked up at him. "How long am I to have the pleasure of your company?"

"Until the baby's born."

"Oh, I see. Keep the little woman quiet and off Ben's back until she's got the baby to keep her quiet and off his back."

Bobby sat down again and leaned forward, lowering his voice. "I would appreciate it very much if you didn't tell Ben I told you."

"I thought you and Ben were friends."

"Well, you know Ben." He said this conspiratorially, as if we shared an intimate knowledge of him. But we didn't. All Ben really showed me was his body. I felt like a whore. My head went light and hot. I put it down in my hand.

Bobby got up. "Did I say something? Are you all right?"

I turned away.

"What have I been telling you! You need fresh air! Exercise! On your feet, little mother," he said, extending his hand.

"You walk and I'll waddle," I told him, as he helped me out of the chair.

***

Bobby joined me in the living room every day after mornings in his office.

Although I was almost overcome with excitement and gratitude at this windfall of his daily presence, to my disappointment and relief he was merely courteous. And why not? As if being in my ninth month of pregnancy was not enough to keep a man at arm's length, I happened also to be married to his boss, who also happened to be none other than Ben Gold, a man who, to put it kindly, would take a rather dim view of anything less than such excruciatingly correct and gentlemanly behavior. Put another way, Bobby would have to be out of his mind, which he most certainly was not.

So we took slow walks around the leafy neighborhood, sometimes without talking, the air between us feeling electric to me, making my heart race. We sat on the couch and looked at the new *Vanity Fair*. I thought I felt him looking at me. We went for drives and attended movie matinees—sometimes our hands would brush. We went to Mass together, neither one of us taking Holy Communion and I took him to services at a Synagogue. He drove me to the doctor for my check-ups, sitting in the waiting room looking at the *Saturday Evening Post* like an expectant father. I liked the way he slowed his long legs to keep in step with me when we walked, and the way his straw skimmer shadowed his face. And his booming laugh in the seat next to me at the movies. The wave in his hair. I noticed the golden hairs on his arm, the blue of his eyes. And his nose. He had, I concluded, a perfect nose. I wondered if my life was making me crazy.

Bobby treated me with the kind of old fashioned gallantry that made you imagine him helping old ladies cross the street, taking a blind man's elbow, catching a child tossed from a burning building. And if he rode the bus, which he never did, you knew he'd be the first one to give up his seat to a lady or an old man. But when he started talking about this girl he had just met, Laura or Lorrie something who studied violin at the Cleveland Institute of Music, I felt such a rush of something like jealously that I had to leave the room. Feeling impossibly fat and hopelessly ugly, I paced the kitchen proceeded by my huge belly, holding a glass of water I couldn't get past my tight throat, telling myself over and over that I was not interested in Bobby Keane. I had enough problems. So why, at the mere mention of this Laura did I get a gnawing, empty place in my midsection like a hit? Why did tears drip down my face? Why was my heart bursting with frustration and anger? And wistfulness? Pacing and sipping the water I finally calmed myself down, but when I came back into the living room I asked Bobby about his time at Cleveland College. I did not want to hear any more about this Laura.

He told me about the Freshman year he spent there and I told him about Windsor Danbury and my scholarship to Ohio State (which I let him think I gave up to marry Ben. I had, after all, some pride). We told each other about our mothers. Bobby talked about his younger brother, Danny, who died of pneumonia at fourteen, and how his mother kept his room like a shrine and all his clothes in the closet. We discussed the Cleveland Indians. Bobby told me about the Schmeling-Stribling fight, we talked about Marlene Dietrich in *Dishonored*, and about the new photoflash bulb that took pictures in the dark. Bobby was crazy about golf and Horton Smith, I was crazy about Amy Johnson because she flew alone half way around the world, and we were both crazy about Garbo. Bobby gave me his copy of *Babbitt*. I told him about Mrs. Shapiro; he asked how bread was baked.

He listened with the kind of attention and understanding women usually have for each other, and when he told me that he had been raised by his mother, aunts, and grandmother, I understood why. I pictured them in the kitchen, telling stories, adoring Bobby, teaching him about the female life by their presence and love. He seemed to hang on my every word, his eyes never leaving my face. But when I spoke to Ben I couldn't tell if he was even listening and his unpredictable moods kept me tense and off balance; when I was with Bobby I felt something tight within me let go. I knew these comparisons were pointless and dangerous. I knew I had to stop them. Besides, I told myself, could this Bobby who does secret stuff with Ben in the basement really be such a do-gooder? Who can't seem to walk past a soup kitchen or bum without giving a handout? (I saw this.) Who goes to church every Sunday? With his mother yet? Why did I think that beneath his cool manner and shady life lay a large and tender heart?

I trembled at the sound of his footstep on the stair. I went from heart-pounding exhilaration to a kind of serene bliss in his presence. I watched him return to his basement with an immense sadness. And I had no idea if what I was feeling was nothing more or less than pregnant hormones. Or confusion and fear. Or love.

So I wrote in my journal about Bobby. I couldn't help it. Even though I knew it could be dangerous, it was as if some powerful force was compelling me. I loved writing his name, describing his clothes, our conversations, the color of his eyes, the way he made me laugh, the graceful way he moved, the way I longed to touch him.

* * *

"Well, how's the redhead today?" Bobby said.

"Stop being so cheerful." I looked at him. "And thin." I rubbed my moist hairline with a damp handkerchief. It was ten days past my due-date and I was bigger than ever.

"Ah hah," he said, rubbing his hands together. "I have my work cut out."

"Don't do me any favors."

"Temper temper."

"And don't call me little mother."

"My mama told me redheads have a terrible temper."

"Oh, shut up." I fanned myself with *Colliers*. I couldn't even read anymore. I couldn't concentrate.

"I know! Let's take a nice walk."

"I can't move."

"A movie. *Possessed* at the Center Mayfield. Joan Crawford."

"I just told you. I can't move."

"I'll be right back," he said. He disappeared and returned with a deck of cards. "Card tricks! Magic! I will entertain and mystify the redhead until she laughs and laughs so hard a little redheaded babe will drop out, plop."

I glared at him.

"Here, cut."

"Can you play hearts?" I asked, brightening. I was pretty good. I used to beat Vivian all the time.

Bobby set up a card table, brought in two dining room chairs and a pencil and score pad. He shuffled the deck like a riverboat gambler.

He beat me four games out of four.

"Red, you're good."

"Good! I'm losing every game! How can you say I'm good?"

"I have to concentrate to beat you."

"Some compliment," I said. "Let's play Honeymoon Bridge."

He beat me three games out of three. He was so good it wasn't fun to play with him. He knew every card I held hand after hand.

"Bobby, are you cheating?"

He raised his hand. "No. I swear on my mother's life. No."

I tossed my cards down.

"I just happen to have a good head for numbers."

"*I* have a good head for numbers. You have a photographic memory."

"Yeah, that's what they call it. That's what I have."

"Really?" I looked at him. "You have a photographic memory?"

"My mind just does it," he said, gathering up the cards. "Since I was a kid."

"You're wasting your talents, Bobby."

"No I'm not. I keep the books and do all the numbers for Ben, didn't you know that?"

"Ben doesn't talk to me about business."

"In fact, that's how we got to know each other—back in '27. Ben was fascinated with the way I could do numbers in my head—he'd give me problems and I'd give him the answers. Then he'd work them on paper and I was always right." He tilted his chair back and put his hands behind his head. "It was a good time-killer back then and God knows we had a lot of time to kill."

A lot of time. Time to kill. I had a sudden terrible stab of insight. "Was this when you were both in jail?"

"Yeah, at the Ohio Pen—" he stopped and turned red.

It had been a shot in the dark. I did not know how I knew. Was it the unborn in my womb whispering with the wisdom gathered from the circular infinity of birth and death? Do unborn babies know the secrets of the ages? Is that why they're born with old, worried faces on their new bodies? But I had no time to dwell on my sudden clairvoyance because I felt a pain so sudden and sharp that I screamed and doubled over as far as my belly would permit.

"Red. Please. I'm sorry. Ben didn't want you to know—"

"Bobby...it's the baby."

Ben and Sam were gone with the Packard. Bobby called Dr. Lear and got my bag that had been packed and ready for three weeks. My water broke in Bobby's Pierce Arrow and soaked my legs and the white leather car seat. With one hand on the wheel, he put the car blanket over me, took his monogrammed handkerchief out of his pocket and wiped my wet face, soaked with tears and sweat. When a contraction made me cry out, he rubbed my back until it passed. His touch was strong and tender and, for a small moment in the pain and delirium of labor, I believed it was Bobby's baby being born. Then he held my hand until we arrived at St. Ann's Hospital, and the Sister at the emergency entrance led me away.

Chapter 8

We named our daughter Margaret Anna; Anna for my mother, and Margaret after Ben's (changing it from Minna.) We called her Maggie. She had hair that felt like silk, skin as soft as air; she smelled of talcum and my own milk. Her hair was dark like Ben's, which disappointed me. I was vain about my hair. People noticed it. I got compliments. But what the hell, I thought. Redheads don't always wind up where they hope they will, either.

Ben had arrived at the hospital with my mother in time for the birth. He stood smiling down at me and the baby, his eyes a radiant amber, while she looked teary and distracted. Her breathing was sad. Even upon the happy occasion of this granddaughter, my mother's breathing emitted a quiet, incalculable sorrow.

I didn't remember Bobby's slip about jail until the next morning when Ben gave me a glittering diamond bracelet and matching brooch. Does the proud new papa steal jewels? Or fence them? Is that how he landed in the slammer? Does he bootleg whisky? I looked at his dark business suit, monogrammed silk tie, and innocent smile and tried to imagine him sitting on his cot behind bars. But I couldn't. All I seemed able to feel was my new maternal flesh. The baby in my arms opened her blue eyes and contemplated me as if she knew I was her mother. Yes, I whispered to her silken cheek, this was no passing thing—we were mother and daughter—the two of us were in it for the long haul. The baby wrapped her tiny fist around my finger and gave a one-sided sloppy smile as if she understood. The nurse said it was gas. But it wasn't. It was a smile. I stared at my baby's perfection as she yawned and stretched. Then she sneezed. We kept on gazing at each other and I felt queer stirrings of an unknown love so pristine and powerful I thought my heart would burst. The warm little body in my arms still seemed somewhere deep within me, deeper even than my heart, and when the nurse lifted her out of my arms I didn't want to let her go. I was afraid she would vanish as suddenly and miraculously and painfully as she had arrived into my reluctant life.

I fell asleep until the nurse brought the baby back again for her feeding. She was a student nurse, about my age, already moving in that brisk, impersonal manner of her profession, her self-confidence crackling the sodden, moist air and thick smells of the hospital room. I watched her gliding in and out of the room in her soundless, immaculately-white shoes and crisp student's uniform, removing my breakfast tray, filling the water pitcher, bringing me clean towels, folding the blanket neatly at the foot of the bed. Feeling a cruel wave of envy, I imagined her dates with boys her own age, her autonomy, her Sunday dinners with proud parents, her sweet freedom—while I was nailed to this bed, pinned down by the soaked Kotex between my legs, this baby sucking my breast, hurting my breast, while my breast kept failing this hungry stranger; this baby would starve to death, I was starving my own child! I burst into tears, the baby began to wail, and looking alarmed, the nurse fled the room.

Ben filled the hospital room with so many flowers the head nurse ordered them moved out at night, muttering something about oxygen. He visited two or three times a day, staring at the baby through the nursery window. Once or twice, as he sat holding my hand, I almost asked him about jail. But I didn't want to get Bobby into trouble. Besides, within the loving husband and adoring father there was also that other raging Ben that I knew too well. So I closed my eyes pretending to sleep so he would leave. That was all I could think of to do. Bobby did not visit me. I did not know if I expected him to. I felt his absence keenly.

Suddenly the baby stopped nursing and began turning a funny shade of blue. Her mouth dropped open. I screamed for the nurse. The student nurse hurried in.

"No!" I screamed. "No! Not you! Get a regular nurse!—a nurse!"

She turned to leave the room. "No! A doctor! My baby! I don't think she's breathing! Run!"

The student nurse ran through the door and in minutes; Dr. Donovan rushed in. He took the baby from my arms and hurried out of the room.

I rang for the nurse. Miss Conrad, the head registered nurse, came in.

"Bring me my clothes! My baby! Something's wrong with my baby! I want to see my baby!"

"Now, Mrs. Gold, you know you're not allowed out of bed. Your baby is in the best of hands," she said soothingly.

"Call my husband!" I screamed.

"Calm down, Mrs. Gold, please. Visiting hours are in ten minutes—he'll be here in ten minutes," she said again, as she left the room.

I got out of bed in my hospital gown and, barefooted, ran down the corridor looking for the doctor and my baby. Miss Conrad suddenly appeared behind me and half carried, half pulled me back to bed.

Ben came into the room, carrying yet another bunch of red roses. "What's wrong? You look terrible."

"The baby! There's something wrong with the baby!"

He turned the color of his eyes—a kind of yellow. "What? What did you say?"

"I don't think she was breathing," I sobbed. "Dr. Donovan took her."

"He took her? Where?"

"I don't know!" I cried.

"I'll get that Donovan," Ben said, turning on his heel with such speed he bumped into the doctor entering the room.

"Where's my baby?" I screamed, getting out of bed again.

"Mrs. Gold, Mr. Gold, please sit down," Dr. Donovan said, gravely, as he pulled up a chair.

Ben stood as if frozen.

"I'm afraid I have bad news," the doctor said.

"No, no, no," I whimpered.

"What," Ben said steadily. "What bad news."

The doctor cleared his throat. "The baby. The baby died. We lost the baby."

"What's this 'we'? Who is this 'we'?" Ben said.

"Mr. Gold, we did everything we could. Everything humanly possible."

"What happened!" I cried.

The doctor turned away from Ben to me quickly, as if in relief. "It looks like she had a heart defect"

"But I felt her kicking in my wife's belly! I felt her!" Ben yelled. "How could she have a heart defect?"

"Heart defects in newborns often aren't revealed until birth."

"So she was okay until birth?" Ben said.

"We won't know for sure until the autopsy—but that's what it looks like now. I'm so sorry," the doctor said.

"So if she was okay until birth, and you were the doctor, it's your fault," Ben shouted, staring yellow-eyed at the doctor. "Maybe you let the cord get wrapped around her neck. Or maybe you let my wife labor too long—over six hours! That could wear the baby's heart out, couldn't it? So why didn't you give her a C-section? You should have given her a C-section!" he yelled, moving toward the doctor until his face was inches away. "Don't lie to me," he hissed, "because I been reading up and you're a goddamn liar."

Dr. Donovan backed away. "I am not lying. I do not lie. I did nothing wrong. I've been delivering babes for over twenty years and all signs point to a heart defect. Tragically, these things do happen," he said, sorrowfully, crossing himself. He looked at me and then at Ben. "As I said, it happens that sometimes heart defects aren't revealed until birth."

"Not to my baby, they don't, Mister Doctor," Ben said, grabbing Dr. Donavan's collar and hitting the side of his head with his fist, knocking him down.

Dr. Donavan yelled, "Help! Tommy! Jim! Help!"

Two big orderlies rushed in and grabbed Ben as the doctor got unsteadily to his feet. A white-coated physician rushed in and helped Dr. Donavan limp from the room while I stood on my knees in bed screaming. After the orderlies released Ben, he began knocking over vases of flowers until they dashed back, seized Ben again, and escorted him out of the hospital.

Chapter 9

Back home, for Ben, it was business as usual. But I stayed in bed unable to move. Or stop crying. After several days, Ben left our bed for the guest room complaining about my weeping, my restlessness, my smell—deep in a well of grief I couldn't get myself out to shower or brush my teeth. Meanwhile, my breasts leaked with milk for my dead baby until Dr. Donavan had a prescription delivered.

I had fallen in love with the baby I hadn't planned on, that I wasn't even sure I wanted. Feeling its busy movements in my womb, I had watched their ripples on my growing abdomen in fascination and curiosity and a swelling love. And when the baby girl I had hoped for was finally born, I held her in my arms, surveyed her exquisite perfection, felt her satin skin against my breast. Then in an instant she was gone, leaving me with a great abyss in my arms, in my *life*. I shrunk into pieces, into shreds, because she had become my heart and left me.

I was going to take her for walks in the beautiful buggy Ben had bought, dress her in the pretty baby clothes folded in the nursery's bureau. I was going to cradle her. My breasts were going to feed her. I was going to put ribbons in her hair. She would change my marriage and my days from fear and bewilderment, to a life of purpose. We were going to be mother and daughter. Mother and daughter! As she grew older I would teach her things; we would be friends. Now Maggie, my daughter, was gone; she was gone, and I wanted to be gone, too, but I didn't know where to go or what to do. I was alone again, in the same confusing place I thought my baby would somehow change. Francine fed me spoonfuls of soup, coaxed me into clean nightgowns, and sat by my side holding my hand as I shook with loss.

I have no idea how long I stayed in bed—it could have been weeks or months. But one day Francine got me into the shower, washed my hair, dressed me, and sat me in the chair. She left and returned with a tray of food—I think it was ham and mashed potatoes—and fed me forkful by forkful. Standing, I felt wobbly and for the next several days Francine linked her arm with mine and walked me around the bedroom. She fed me coffee, more of her nourishing food, and finally got me steadily to my feet.

I came downstairs, scrubbed, sweet-smelling, brushed and nicely dressed, right back where I had started. Ben and Sam greeted me warmly—Sam kissed my cheek and Ben gave me his dazzling smile in relief at my final presence. He pulled me toward him, obviously eager for the sex he had missed during my last months of pregnancy and the long time I'd spent in bed. "We'll have more babies," he whispered in my ear.

"Where's Bobby?" I said, moving away.

"In the office. Francine told me you were coming down for lunch so Sam and I came up to celebrate." There was a bottle of champagne in a silver bucket on the table, and Ben opened it with great panache sending the cork shooting across the room like a missile. He poured three glasses in the grand style of the wine steward at the Stork Club.

Bobby didn't join us for lunch and, to my frustration and relief, he stayed in his office all day. As usual, overcoated men in fedoras came and went in singles and pairs; there were the same muffled movements and voices in the basement offices and Bobby stayed out of sight. The Packard with Sam at the wheel and Ben in the back disappeared regularly, sometimes with Bobby along. Everything was so routine in the basement and household, it was almost as if Bobby's slip about jail existed only in my own disturbed imagination. My pretty dresses fit me again and there were more of those nights at Allie's—eating, drinking, listening to jazz, while Ben did his usual tablehopping as I sat with Sam watching faces lift to Ben with that respectful earnestness people give to men of power. Everything seemed the same as before.

But it wasn't. My life after Maggie was now unfocused and blurred, as if it had been lived by someone else. I had never imagined myself a mother, but now, after Maggie's birth and death, it was as if I had never been anything else, and I saw with an awful clarity and not a little self-contempt what a child, a coward, I had been, regressing from being my mother's mother to my husband's child, seduced by glittering dresses and Ben's secrets and a vision of escape from my mother's life. I felt as if I was recovering from a long illness—of will, of spirit, of my very being; I wanted to belong to myself again. And as if Maggie had wrapped her small fist around my finger and dragged me into adulthood, I was now ready to confront my husband and his anger for the truth.

I wrote in my journal for long stretches of time about Ben's, Sam's, and Bobby's routine. Nothing escaped my eye; the hour they left in the Packard, who was driving, when it returned. I observed the times Bobby went along. I noted that they left the house on Mondays and Thursdays, and that the overcoated men came on Tuesdays and

Wednesdays and never before three in the afternoon. I eavesdropped in their basement offices, pretending to get some canned peaches from the pantry, but I couldn't make any sense of the few words I was able to hear.

It was time—well overtime—to demand the truth. But when? Not when Ben was hurrying downstairs to his office, or leaving the house. And not before making love, or afterward either, because he always fell asleep; and certainly not at mealtime or when he had been drinking, which he did every night except Sunday; and of course not with Sam or Bobby present, and I knew enough not to confront him during the many days when he was grim and unapproachable.

Still, although it was true that Ben was busy and remote, I had discovered that his routine was as predictable as our mailman's. Except for his lovemaking, which was impulsive and could occur anywhere and at any time—on the floor, in the shower, standing up in his perfect clothes closet, on Francine's day off in the kitchen with my back cool against the ice box—there was a structure to his days and nights that was as precise as his clothes hanging in his closet. He spent the weekends with me; Friday and Saturday we went to Allie's, and unless there was a telephone call, he was always home on Sunday. He had breakfast exactly at ten minutes after eight, served by Francine who knew how he liked his morning newspaper folded (once in the center, so he could see the entire headline), his coffee (black with one teaspoon of sugar), his eggs (over lightly), his toast (almost burned). Lunch was at twelve on the dot always consisting of Francine's homemade vegetable soup, a pastrami sandwich on rye with mustard, and hot tea in a glass, which he sipped through a cube of sugar in his mouth as his father had done. He never drank alcohol during working hours. I even came to notice that his involvement with me was scheduled. He became attentive during dinner, asking about my day, and while dressing in the morning, talking to me while I struggled awake—he only slept four or five hours a night—pulling the draperies open on their silken cord, commenting on the weather, describing the colors of the sky or the shape of a cloud, encouraging me to invite my mother for dinner and a Sunday drive, charming me once more with his energy's heat and the beauty of his smile. If it was raining, he would stand transfixed, as if nailed there by the driving rain slamming against the windows. Once during a violent electrical storm with savage flashes of lightning stabbing the air, he turned to me from the window with a flushed face, glittering eyes, and a canny misshapen smile, breathing as fast as if he had been running. He composed himself and the moment passed, but I felt shaken, as if I had caught him in some kind of private consummation that I should not have seen.

One morning there was a sudden violent storm blowing down from

Canada, whipping fifty-mile icy winds off Lake Erie. We stared at the white dervishes of swirling snow and the startling decent of the window thermometer to twenty-five degrees below zero, while the radio droned on about power failures, school closings, business cancellations, babies born unattended at home, snow-covered cars stuck and abandoned, stranded motorists, deaths. It was a deserted world, as if a giant hand had covered all of life with the white of shrouds. Ben watched quietly from the window, standing so motionlessly he seemed to me subdued, defeated, as if hopelessly outmatched by nature's violence.

I liked to watch him dress. Even coming out of the shower, even putting on his socks and underwear and buttoning his shirt, he moved with that easy grace you see in movie stars or athletes. Then, meticulously dressed and scented, his face gleaming, his hair shining black, his skin smelling of soap and piney aftershave, before going out for his newspaper, he bent down dutifully to kiss me goodbye, like a regular husband leaving for the bus. It reassured and worried me. It made me uneasy. It made me feel that I did not know him, would never know him; he had too many moods, too many parts, too many roles, while I, transparent as glass, was lost in confusion.

Once Ben told me that in spite of his strong sex drive he had never been able to be promiscuous. He said he had always had only one girlfriend at a time and that very few women attracted him in that way. He had never been able to perform in a whorehouse, he said, with anyone that was not of the Jewish faith, or with a woman who had had a lover before him. He did not know why this was so. He told me this when he came home late one night, the smell of alcohol oozing from his pores; he told me after he had awakened me to make love; he told me almost in apology. Listening, I understood why I had fit the bill.

There was a phonograph in the living room with a trumpet speaker and on Sunday nights after dinner, Ben would wind it up and play records from his collection of opera arias. He had a particular favorite, "Soave Fanculla" from Puccini's *La Boheme* that he would play over and over, patiently cranking the handle when it ran down, filling my ears with its scratchy, hollow sound until I had to leave the room. But Ben sat listening with his eyes closed, a small smile on his face, nodding his head and making little arcs with his hand in time to the music.

Well, tomorrow was Sunday. This was my time, I decided, a time as good as any and better than most. Tomorrow night I would stay and face the music, I thought, without smiling at my stupid pun to myself.

After I finally fell asleep that night, I woke every hour during the long night, waking again and again, as if for an unknown appointment, as if I were expecting someone. Was it my own self I was anticipating? I had been living as if my life belonged to my husband; I did not know how it happened. I had not meant to give it away like that. Now, I wanted it back. I saw that I had lived with Ben for a year in an unspoken conspiracy; we were a perfect fit—he didn't want to tell me the truth and I didn't want to hear it. I became aware of all this without words in one of those moments when the mind, suspended between sleep and waking, becomes swollen and ripe with unexpected insight.

I wanted to record that newfound wisdom, got my journal from its hiding place, and wrote.

CHAPTER 10

It did not turn out as I had planned. Not at all. I should have waited until he finished listening to his music, until he was relaxed; I should not have blurted it out like that the minute we left the dinner table.

I had decided to dress up, trying on three or four outfits before choosing a dress of green silk with a low neckline. I knew Ben liked me in green. I knew it set off my hair. I put on makeup and my emerald earrings. Ankle-strap shoes with high heels. I was not unlearned in the feminine arts.

We had dinner at eight. Ben was languid and affable as he usually was on Sunday nights, looking forward, as he said, to a quiet evening of dinner and music. After Francine cleared away the coffee cups and dessert dishes, Ben dabbed at his mouth with his napkin, pushed his chair away from the table, and with a satisfied sigh, headed for his record cabinet in the living room.

"I want to talk to you," I said.

"So talk," he said, going through his records.

"Sit down," I said.

He glanced over his shoulder at me, looking amused. Then he balanced a record carefully with both hands upright on its edges, put it on the turnstile, and began turning the crank.

"Put the record down. I want to talk to you," I said again. Then I said, "Please."

Still looking amused and indulgent, he sat down on the edge of his chair and folded his hands like an obedient schoolboy. "How's this?"

"I want to know what you're doing."

He looked puzzled. "What I'm doing?"

"Yes! What you're doing! I want to know!" I cried.

"Why, I'm doing what I was told, I'm sitting down," he said, with an infuriating smile on his face. Then he got up and started cranking the gramophone again.

I had expected to make him mad, not amused. "I'm your wife! I want to know what's going on around here!" I cried, my voice raised into a kind of crackling shout that was definitely not what I had rehearsed. Bracing for his fury, I watched his face, but he looked merely surprised. Then in the space of an instant his eyes turned into yellow stones and his smile changed, stretching, pulling his lips back, exposing his teeth. I heard Francine clattering in the kitchen. I heard the big clock ticking on the mantle. I could smell the pot roast I had been unable to eat. We were faced off—Ben staring at me as if I was foaming at the mouth or something, my eyes fastened on his killing glare, my face hot, the room breathing like something alive.

Suddenly Sam came pounding up the steps from the basement and lumbered into the room, breaking into our locked stare. Seeing me sitting there, he stopped short. "Kate, I need to talk to Ben. Alone," he said, looking at me hard. But I settled back into my chair and folded my arms.

"What's up?" Ben said, without taking his eyes from my flaming face.

Sam's suit looked as if he'd been sleeping in it. But then it always did. Even in his tuxedo at Allie's, or at a favorite speakeasy in New York, he'd hike up his tuxedo pants, or spill scotch on his tie, food in his lap, or self-consciously keep pulling on his lapels to straighten his jacket, as if he knew he and his tuxedo were incompatible. "You're such a klutz," Ben would say.

"I have to talk to you," Sam said again.

"Speak freely," Ben said, still glaring at me. "We are in the presence of my wife as she so enlightened me a moment ago. It seems, Sam, it appears, Sam, that she insists on full disclosure, that my wife, that the little woman here, does not appreciate her husband's efforts to protect her from the grim realities of real life, or for that matter, it also appears that my wife also does not appreciate her husband's efforts to provide her not only the aforementioned protection, but with all the necessities and yes, may I so modestly admit, a few small luxuries now and then, some jeweled goodies here and there, a few fur coats to keep her nice and snug during the winter winds. All of which no doubt she forces herself to enjoy a little. So speak, Sam please. My wife wishes to be spared nothing."

Sam glanced doubtfully at me. "Ben, you're *meshugener* if you want me to talk in front of her..."

"Excuse me for interrupting, Sam, but I see that my wife has not forgotten how to blush," Ben went on, his eyes still fastened on my hot face. "Does this suggest to you that perhaps she could be a little bit aware of opening a rather large can of worms?" He glared at me a moment longer, and then to my immense relief finally turned to Sam. "So what's up?"

"They did it again. The Sarsenis did it again," Sam said, sitting down and jiggling his foot. I had never seen him so agitated.

"Where?"

"Just over the border. We got *tsuris* now, big time.""

"Which truck?"

"The Mack. Those *goys* Tony and Frank gave it up without a fight! They just handed it over!"

"Calm down and lower your voice. They were doing what they were told."

"I know what they were told," Sam said. "It was a mistake what they were told. This's all Bobby's fault. Why do you listen to that *meshuge* kid?" He was shaking his leg like a small boy who had to go to the bathroom. "Now look what happened. The goddamn *gonefs*!"

"How much was on it?"

"Fifty cases of beer, sixty-five whisky. That makes, let's see, a hundred-sixty beer and a hundred-fifty whisky they got in three hijackings. Plus three of our trucks."

"Bootlegging!" I said. They both looked at me twice, doing a kind of double take.

"Bobby's on his way," Sam said, getting up.

"You sent for him on a Sunday night for another hijacking?"

"You're the one always wants him. I'd just as soon keep him out of this. He's nothing but a pain in the ass." Sam glanced at me. "Excuse me. Anyway, that ain't the half of it," he said, sighing and sitting down again.

"Go on."

"Mario Sarseni and two of his boys go over to Midnight Johnny's. Mario sticks a rod in Johnny's ribs and tells him from now on he's buyin' from the Sarseni brothers, startin' now." He got up and started to pace. "The goddamn gall! Our booze—our truck—our speak. Johnny Midnight's ours!"

"What did Johnny do?"

Sam almost moaned. "What do you think he did? He had a rod in his ribs. Anyways, what does he care who the hell he pays as long as he gets his booze."

There were footsteps on the basement stairs, not heavy and pounding like Sam's, but light, quick. The three of us looked up as Bobby came striding into the room wearing a tuxedo.

"Well, well, if it isn't the college boy in his monkey suit," Sam said.

Bobby pointed a slim finger at me. "She's here—"

"The little lady wishes to be informed. Sit down, Bobby."

Frowning, Bobby sat down on the couch next to Sam and glanced at me. "So what's the big problem?"

Ben moved forward in his chair. "The Sarseni brothers hijacked our Mack again and sold the score to Johnny with the help of a rod and his two gorillas."

Bobby whistled. Then he was silent.

"Cat got your tongue?" Sam said.

"Sorry." Bobby cleared his throat. "I'm just not used to seeing Kate here like this. You said—"

"For Christ sake," Ben said, "we got a real problem here. Do you think you could keep your mind on the goddamn subject?"

I noted numbly to myself that I had never seen Ben as tight-lipped and venomous. I looked at Bobby's cold-eyed, narrowing expression layered over the wide blue eyes and open face I knew. What was happening here? Who were these people?

Bobby shook his head slowly. "I never figured it. I never figured those punks would have that kind of nerve."

"You were wrong," Sam said. "Ben said you were wrong. We shouldn't have listened to you." He had stopped jiggling his leg and was sitting straight with his hands on his big thighs like a rumpled executive. I had forgotten how small and hairy his hands were.

Bobby turned to Ben. "Look at it this way," he said, "it's the cost of doing business. We can afford it. It's okay."

"It's not okay," Ben said. "Not anymore."

"Ben, there's enough business for everyone," Bobby said. Sitting calmly in his tuxedo, patent leather shoes and spats, next to the rumpled, agitated Sam, he looked oddly misplaced. Or so I wanted to believe. I wondered where Bobby had been, all dressed up, with what lady. If they had made love. I shifted in my chair. Isn't it enough that I'm getting an earful of my husband's miserable secrets? Do I have to torment myself with Bobby's sex life, too? But I sat there thinking about some gorgeous woman wrapped around Bobby's golden body.

"Who the hell you think you're dealing with here, fraternity brothers?" Ben was saying, his cat's eyes fastened on Bobby. "These are the Sarseni brothers, the roughest bastards in the business."

"All the more reason not to start up with them."

Listening to murders being discussed like ordinary business deals of, say, office furniture, or cooking stoves, I became unnerved by my own stupidity. How could I have lived in this house and not known it was a house of death? Still, I did know. I knew. But now I saw that I had been a child playing house in beautiful grown-up clothes and a fantasy of rescue, until my dead baby somehow made a woman out of me.

Ben got up from his chair. "You think I'm going to let those punks push me out? Three times I warned them. And this is their answer. I threatened, now I got to do it. Or I'm done. They'll eat me alive."

"We got to hit 'em," said Sam, his eyes as unmoving as a fish's.

"Let's have them worked over first. We can always go for the hit," Bobby said.

"Look. Bobby. I'm trying not to lose my patience here," Ben said. Unless he fell into one of his shouting rages, Ben's voice was modulated, and yet so threatening it demanded the kind of attention you would be crazy to ignore. A person in conversation with Ben was made to sound kind of puny against the quiet power of his voice.

"You're an amateur and amateurs get knocked out fast in this business," Ben went on. "The cemetery's full of amateurs. I listened to you before and it cost me. I'm not making the same mistake twice. You stick to the books and leave this part of the business to me."

"Stop patronizing me," Bobby said

Ben extracted a cigarette from the monogrammed silver case in his coat pocket and Sam got up and lit it with his thumbnail on a kitchen match. Ben smoked quietly while we all sat silently watching. There was a kind of tragic solemnity in the room as if sitting in your chair, you were already attending the funerals. Ben rarely smoked in the house so the act was some kind of signal that caused our expectant attention.

"Okay, college boy, I'll explain," Ben said. "We can't work them over. They're waiting for us. It's a trap. They expect us to go for the hit because that's what they'd do. They're lookin' for a war. They want to knock us out. They want our sources, our territory, our trucks, customers, speaks, our cops, everything. We'd never get close enough to work them over without getting plugged."

"Then how can you hit them?" Bobby asked.

"By being smarter. Which I am."

"How?"

"Sam and I'll work out the plan. You stay out of it. It's not your department."

Bobby leaned forward. "Ben, listen. Maybe now's the time to get out. Go legit. I've been working on this plan—"

"Ben, time's running out," Sam said, getting up. "We got to move."

"Let him talk," Ben said. He turned to Bobby. "Keep it short."

"First, we stop running booze and open a speakeasy—let the other guys get their brains blown out. We can fix it up, put in tables, a dance floor, a good kitchen. We'll clean up. Texas Guinan cleared seven hundred thousand in the last ten months."

"Yeah. And Waxey Gordon made over a million running hooch from Canada," Ben said.

"He also almost got himself killed a couple times," Bobby said. "I figure our cost at around thirteen-hundred-fifty a month, which includes four-hundred to the feds, cops, and the DA's office, and another forty for Danny Archer—"

"Who's Danny Archer?"

"The cop on the beat. Food and booze'll clear around fifty thousand a month."

"Ben—" Sam said. "We gotta go."

"Shut up, Sam. I'm not through," Bobby said, still looking at Ben. "There's a building on Chester Avenue for sale really cheap. We buy it and keep on buying buildings cheap that were hit by the depression." He leaned back on the couch. "Then when Repeal comes we wind up owning half of downtown Cleveland. Plus a good restaurant. Legitimately."

"They been talkin' Repeal a long time," Sam said. "It's just talk."

"I'm telling you, Ben, it's coming," Bobby said. "Times are so bad Hoover'll get beat and every bootlegger in the country'll be out of business overnight."

"Listen to him," Sam said. "Soon as things get a little hot, college boy wants out."

"Ben," Bobby said, talking fast, "let the Sarsenis and the Murphys and the Ciccones and the Levines kill each other off. Let's get out."

"I'll think about it."

"They could hit you, too, you know," Bobby said.

"Not if we move fast and smart."

"We've done enough talking," Sam said, moving over to the basement door.

"Yeah," Ben said, getting up.

Bobby stood.

"Not you, Bobby." Ben turned to me, sitting stunned in my chair. "And, my dear wife, I think you've heard enough for one night." He hurried from the room, Sam following. I heard their feet pound down the basement steps and then the office door slam shut. The living room was still.

And so I was baptized by an ocean's six-foot swell that made me grab onto my chair. Bobby was still standing where Ben left him. I looked at him imploringly, a foreigner lost in a grotesque land. My husband was not going to murder anybody. That was ridiculous. He bootlegged, yes. Sure. Okay. That's what he did. But he was not going to murder these Sarseni people. No. "Bobby, I—"

But he shook his head, avoiding my eyes, and left the room without a word, closing the front door behind him.

I had been sitting quietly during the meeting moving my head from one to the other like a spectator at a bizarre tennis match. My foot had fallen asleep. I took off my shoe and sat in the chair rubbing it. I heard a faucet drip in the kitchen and the ticking clock. I heard my own pulse in my ears.

I had long since learned that Sam was Ben's right hand and alter ego. He was like his shadow; a grotesque butler and chauffeur who, I now saw, could turn himself into a hit man at Ben's will. When Ben was in his office, Sam waited patiently for him in the basement reception room, leafing through the *Saturday Evening Post* or *Colliers*. Except for the times when Ben and I were alone in our bedroom, it was as if I had married two men joined at the hip.

Rubbing my foot, trying to fathom what I had just heard, I realized that Sam performed or arranged the business of murder, a job description that foolishly had never occurred to me. Of course! Sam and Ben's attachment was bound with the glue of murder. Still, unlike other killers, they were no danger to each other. Ben gave the orders, Sam followed them faithfully, his loyalty obviously tested by Ben and earned.

I stood up stiffly. Moving like a sleepwalker, I went upstairs to the guest room, stretched out on the bed, and closed my eyes. Then I thought I was floating in the rocking chair with Maggie in my arms, lost in a sea of salt-water tears. I never wanted you to have a killer for a father, I explained to Maggie. But Maggie had vanished. Maggie, Maggie, Maggie, I silently called. Then I saw my baby's body floating away.

Waking, I looked at my watch. one AM. The house was quiet. Bobby. I've got to talk to Bobby. I opened the door slowly, a crack at a time. Moving silently down the hall, I stood in the doorway of our bedroom until my eyes adjusted and I could see that Ben was in bed snoring softly. I crept slowly down the stairs to the kitchen telephone.

But I didn't know Bobby's telephone number. The telephone book was in the top drawer and I clawed at its pages, certain the number would be unlisted. But almost weeping with relief I found his name: there it was in black and white, Robert Joseph Keane, 8021 Mercer Dr., 9441.

"What number please," the operator said.

"9441," I hissed, looking over my shoulder.

"Speak up please," the operator sang.

I turned and faced the doorway. "9. 4. 4. 1," I said softly, the mouthpiece pressed against my lips.

"Thank you."

I heard the operator ringing through the pounding in my head.

"Hello?" Bobby answered at last, sounding guarded.

"Bobby. It's Red," I whispered.

"What? Who is this?"

"Red. It's Red."

"Red?"

Silence. A long silence on the wire. My body grew heavy holding itself up.

"I have to talk to you," I said in my stage whisper.

"Where's Ben?"

"Upstairs."

"He's home? He's upstairs? Are you crazy?"

"He's sleeping."

"You're insane calling me like this."

"Bobby—please—I have to talk to you—"

"Get back upstairs," Bobby whispered, as if Ben was upstairs in his house, too.

"But I have to talk to you," I said again.

"Call me tomorrow night after they leave. I'll meet you somewhere." And he hung up.

* * *

I fell into an exhausted sleep in the guest room that night.

Ben came in the next morning, waking me. "I won't be home for dinner," he said. "I'll tell Francine." He smiled at me like an ordinary husband discussing a business engagement, as if I hadn't just heard his grisly scheme, as if it was only my own appalling imagination that was tormenting me. "Why don't you take your mother to Schrafft's for a nice dinner?" he said, kissing me goodbye, as if I had slept in our bed instead of in the guest room in my clothes, as if nothing had changed.

Looking out the window I watched Ben hurry back from the newsstand with the *Plain Dealer* under his arm. He dashed into the Packard, where Sam was waiting at the wheel, and they roared off with the car door still open.

Ben didn't come back for his lunch, which Francine finally cleared away. I spent the day dressed and waiting until at last a friendly darkness lowered itself over the spring twilight like an arrived accomplice.

I called upstairs to Francine that I was going out for dinner with my mother. Then I hurried into the kitchen and called Bobby.

"Hello," he said, on the first ring.

"They're gone," I said.

"I'll pick you up on the corner of Wendover and Claremont in twenty minutes."

Chapter 11

Almost running to meet Bobby, I reached the street corner a full ten minutes early. The night had settled softly after the rain, and the air felt moist and fragrant with spring. Waiting, looking at the houses with their warmly lit, aloof windows, I wondered what it felt like to be inside those rooms, safe and calm. Finally, watching and pacing under the early budding of April trees, I saw the silver Pierce Arrow turn the corner of Wendover Drive and come toward me.

Bobby pulled over to the curb and I climbed in. He was unshaven, rumpled.

"Are you all right?" he asked. "You look terrible."

I laughed. I couldn't help it. "I was just thinking the same thing about you."

He pulled the car away from the curb without smiling.

"Where are we going?" I asked.

"Manhattan Ballroom."

"We're going dancing?" I said, still smiling, feeling absurdly relieved sitting next to Bobby.

"It just happens to be the most inconspicuous place I can think of to park—they're having a marathon tonight."

I closed my eyes imagining we were contestants with nothing to think about or worry about or do except cling together and keep moving, holding each other up the way I had seen in the newsreels, our only world the dance floor, the music, the few remaining, staggering couples; life made exquisitely simple for days and nights, for as long as the music lasted.

"Thanks for coming out, thanks for seeing me," I said.

He nodded without speaking or looking at me. I glanced at his closed, unshaven face. This was not the Bobby I knew, the Bobby of my daydreams. We drove in silence. I hadn't been inside his car since the night Maggie was born, the night my water broke all over the seat. Now the car smelled of polished leather, it smelled clean, rich. When I was home with my mother there would be an occasional car like this go by the bakery or pass as I went to school; a car so beautiful it turned heads, stopping conversation. People stared wistfully at the couple inside, imagining their lives to be as invulnerable to illness, poverty, and unpleasant surprises as the gods—how else could they possess such a thing? And now I was inside, riding in the silver Pierce Arrow with a man as handsome and rich as a movie star, and I found myself longing to be the person I was then, staring from the sidewalk. How could I—how could everyone—be so wrong?

We arrived at a long, low, flat-roofed building that looked like a warehouse. A blue neon figure of a dancing couple flashed on and off under a red, white, and blue banner that read MANHATTAN BALLROOM. I could hear the band playing "Alexander's Ragtime Band," slowly, heavily. Bobby parked the Pierce Arrow between a Ford and Essex, turned off the lights and motor, and sat staring out into the night. A cloud had drifted over the risen moon and except for the music drifting out of the building, the car was quiet and dark.

"Ben and Sam left over an hour ago," I said.

He nodded. He had barely spoken since he picked me up.

"Will he really do it?"

"Do what?"

I looked at him. "You know what."

"Sorry," Bobby said, shifting in his seat. "I'm not used to direct questions in such matters."

I waited for him to say no it was just talk. Or, of course he won't do it. But he just sat there looking out the window. Now someone was singing "My Melancholy Baby," in a thin-voiced tenor.

"Look, you were sitting there, you heard him," he finally said.

"Yes, but you know Ben," I said, still hoping.

"Don't you?"

"Not that way."

Bobby sighed. "The answer is yes, I think he'll really do it." He rubbed his forehead. "Well, that is, he'll have it done."

"Same thing."

He looked up. "Same thing."

"I can't believe it."

"Then don't ask me."

"Has he...murdered before?" I whispered.

"I don't know."

"Have you?"

He stared at me. "I think you know the answer to that," he said bitterly.

After waiting all day to be alone with him, practically the first thing out of my mouth was an insult. Ashamed, I wanted to reach for his hand. But I didn't. I just said, "I'm sorry." Everything was different, wrong.

Bobby sighed and turned to me. "Look, we're both upset."

Now a woman was singing, "Dream a Little Dream of Me" in a tired monotone and I closed my eyes, listening. The song reminded me of Mary Ann Kelly, my best friend before I transferred to Windsor Danbury and met Vivian. Mary Ann was small and sharp-faced and liked to sing along with the radio in a nice husky voice while I tried to do my homework. Mary Ann liked to come to my house after school because my mother wasn't home and she could read her movie magazines, listen to the radio, try out different hairdos, smoke cigarettes, pluck and pencil her eyebrows copying those of Marlene Dietrich from *Silver Screen Magazine* propped up on her school notebook—all of which Mrs. Kelly forbade. Mary Ann had an amazing knowledge of cosmetics; she knew about cleansing creams, night creams, hand lotions. She knew all the lipstick colors at Woolworth's from Ruby to Cardinal and from Flame to Cherry; colors I couldn't even tell apart. She knew the various staying powers of face powders, choosing, after much experimentation, Coty's, in its flowered box. And now, inexplicably, Mary Ann was the one going to college, to Flora Stone Mather, one of the best women's colleges in the country, which I discovered when I ran into her downtown one Saturday. We went to the drug store for a cherry coke (like the old days, Mary Ann said) while she talked about her courses of study, her favorite professors, her schedule, her friends, her work on the yearbook. We had mysteriously changed places; Mary Ann now the committed and serious student, planning to teach literature, she said, on the college level, while I, sipping my coke, felt envious and bewildered and suddenly too hot in the blue suit and furs and cloche that covered my ears, while Mary Ann looked comfortable and years younger in a sweater and skirt. We parted with hugs and promises to keep in touch, knowing we would not.

Now, the orchestra switched to "April Showers" which still managed to sound like "Dream a Little Dream of Me," played as it was in the same tempo. I felt Bobby looking at me.

"I knew Ben was up to something," I said, "but I never figured on—on—murder."

"So what did you have to sit there and listen for?"

"For the truth."

"The truth stinks."

"So I found out.

"You were better off not knowing."

"Why were you in jail?" I blurted out.

He hesitated. Then he said, "Auto theft. First offense. One to three."

"You stole cars?"

He looked away. "Car," he mumbled. "One lousy car." He slid down in his seat. "I was going to Cleveland College, working at Joey's Diner nights. So one day after work I see this gorgeous black Essex with the key in the ignition, just waiting there at the curb. I was caught twenty minutes later. I paid for that little joyride with seven months, two weeks, three days, and four and a half hours in the Ohio Pen. Counting time off for good behavior."

"And that's when you met Ben."

"Yeah."

"What was he in for?"

"Wheelman for an armed robbery. He was working for Frank Genosa then. Genosa was running whisky from Canada, but he was so stupid he never saw what a gold mine it could be—he'd actually go out and hold up stores between trips. So a cop on the beat collars Genosa red-handed while he's sticking up this grocery store. Ben was waiting in the car with the motor running so he got away, but Genosa turned stoolie and informed on him in a plea bargain. They arrested Ben and sent him up for fourteen months—actually eight counting good time."

He looked at his watch.

"Go on," I said.

He shook his head. "I better get you home," he said, reaching for the ignition key.

I understood that his reluctance to talk was more for himself than me. I understood that he was ashamed and knew that Ben would not be. I touched his arm. "Bobby, we're friends. Nothing can change that."

He turned to me and smiled. It was a wistful smile. I thought I saw his eyes glisten. He cleared his throat.

He looked so earnest, his blond head so pale and eager, I had to stop myself from touching his face. "Go on," I said again.

He looked at me. "You're sure you want to hear all this?"

Later I thought I should have said no, please take me home now, I've heard quite enough, thank you very much. But I said I'm sure. I said tell me. Call it curiosity or survival or falling in love or growing up or reaching the point of no return. But I had to know.

"I've never told this stuff to anyone," he said, his hands on the steering wheel. I expected him to start the car and drive me home, but he took a deep breath and turned to me. "You know that saga of the widowed mother who cleans offices at night so her son can go to college? And the rotten son lets her down, goes bad, breaks her heart? It's a classic, a cliché—you've seen the movie a hundred times. Except that's what happened. I got sent up and broke my mother's heart. How corny can you get?" It was too dark to see his face, but his voice tightened as if his throat closed on him. Then he started talking again and told me the story.

"They put me in the same cell with Ben, who had three months left to serve. We passed the time playing cards and doing those number games—Ben gave me difficult math problems and I worked them in my head. Genosa, who had informed on Ben, had been sent up for ten to twenty for a fourth offense, and Ben was itching to get out and take over his customers and suppliers before guys like Nig Rosen and Moe Dalitz moved in. Ben said he could use someone with a photographic memory and talent for numbers and offered me a job when I got out. With the right organization, Ben said, there was big money to be made—Bugsy Siegel and Meyer Lansky were making a fortune trucking whisky down from Canada, and Dutch Schultz and Lucky Luciano were cleaning up running booze out of the Bahamas through Charleston.

"Four months later, when I was paroled," Bobby went on, "Ben had already bought a truck, hired Sam to ride shotgun, and was running whisky down from Canada once a week. He bought a second truck when I joined them, and in less than three years we had four trucks, Macks and Reos, and nine speakeasies for our booze, mostly supplied by the Bronfman brothers in Montreal. Ben hires the drivers," Bobby said, "and takes care of the speakeasies and suppliers—he's now working on some additional sources in Cuba. I handle the money, do the payroll, and take care of payoffs to politicians and cops.

"And there's not a scrap of evidence," he said, "not a politician's name or a cop's name, or a place, or a date, or a number that's recorded anywhere. It's all in here," he said, pointing to his head. He shifted his narrow body. "In six years Ben and I went from being broke ex-cons to businessmen with an operation as well run and efficient as any corporation." He grinned. "And much more profitable."

"Swell. Good for you and Ben."

"Look, Prohibition's a stupid law, an unenforceable law. Our business is simply supply and demand, pure capitalism, what's more American? All we do is give the folks what they want."

"Including murder?"

He looked off somewhere in the middle distance. "You heard me try to talk him out of it."

"I also heard how he wasn't talked out of it."

He turned to me and lowered his voice. "I'm going to tell you something because I trust you. I want no part of this. It wasn't in the job description. I'm getting out."

"To open the speakeasy?"

He shook his head. "If I'm on my own, I'd rather go legit and get into real estate. But I'm not telling Ben until the last minute. He won't like it because his business is all in my head and he doesn't trust anybody." He looked at his watch and straightened up in his seat. "I shouldn't have kept you out this long." He glanced at me. "Or told you so much." I thought I saw his face color.

So Bobby was in jail. But who am I to judge, I told myself. We had both stumbled into Ben's life. The difference was that he was getting out and I didn't seem to know how. I hated him for leaving. I envied him. I dreaded his absence. But looking at his solemn profile, I also felt a vicarious and wistful thrill for his escape into a life free of Ben.

"Where did you tell Ben you were going?" he asked, starting the car.

"My mother's."

"What if he calls her?"

"She doesn't have a phone."

Driving back to the street corner Bobby seemed talked out, drained. We rode without saying a word, but when we arrived I sat there next to him, unable to move, already feeling his absence from my life. He finally said goodnight Kate, without looking at me. Getting out of the car, I felt a rush of something like loss, and watching Bobby drive away I thought I felt my soul empty. I stood at the street corner until the Pierce Arrow disappeared, leaving no trace, as if I had imagined it. The houses were dark now, the trees vanished into the black night, and walking home I made up my mind. I would tell Ben not to do this thing. There was a way to stop him. I was sure of it. After all, Ben wasn't a monster, a murderer, he was my husband—look how he had adored Maggie—and in his way, he loved me. He had a side to him that was difficult, of course, he had a temper, he could be stubborn, but wasn't there another side to him, as well? The loving father and generous husband. The lover of children. The kind employer and good friend. Francine, Sam, and Bobby had been with him for years. And didn't Ben love music? Would a murderer love music? Would a music-lover murder? Of course not. Besides, Bobby could be wrong—Ben could have cooled off by now and changed his mind. I imagined Ben telling me with his beautiful smile, don't be silly I just lost my temper. Of course I wouldn't murder anybody. Sometimes Sam gets me going like that, but I always calm down.

I went upstairs and saw that Ben still wasn't home. I went into the guest room, stretched out on the bed, and fell into a deep sleep for the first time in two days.

Chapter 12

"I want to talk to you," Ben said.

Waking, I looked at him standing over me in his blue silk pajamas. In my dream I had been afraid of his neon-yellow pupils. I closed my eyes, but I was aware that I was being steadily stared at by a man who calmly arranges murders. I jumped up, alert and trembling. I was still in my clothes.

"What time is it?"

"Six-thirty," he said."

I hurried into our bedroom, Ben following, and went into the bathroom. When I came out after my shower wrapped in my robe, he was in bed. He smiled at me.

"Come here, Kate," he said, his head deep in the pillow, his smile slow.

"I thought you wanted to talk," I said.

"Later."

"No," I said. "Now."

"Come here, Kate," he said again, looking at me, still smiling.

"Later," I said, mimicking him. "I want to talk to you."

He sat up in bed. "You didn't get an earful already? You want to know, you ask questions that are none of your business, you stick your nose in a private meeting, a business meeting, you sleep in the guest room two nights. Enough already. I want you to come to bed, Kate. Now."

I shook my head. "I'm too upset."

"Yeah," he said. "The Sarsenis. The bastards."

"Ben, if you care about me, our marriage, if you cared about our baby, you won't—do—it," I said, my voice trailing off, unable to utter the unthinkable word through the swelling in my throat.

"Kate, I don't like being told how to run my business. You know that. I think you know that."

"I'm telling Maggie's father and my husband not to be a—a— murderer," I said, my voice thin as thread. I noticed that my hands were trembling, and I walked over to the window. Outside, the trees were turning their winter branches into a newborn green. I could make out our next-door neighbors at their breakfast table and imagined their corn flakes and orange juice, their safe, steady lives.

I felt Ben's arms around my waist. "Kate," he said, breathing my name. "Let's not do this, let's not fight." He kissed my neck. "Come to bed with me. Please."

I shook my head, my wet fists in my pockets.

He dropped his arm. "Why are you doing this to me? Things were good with us, everything was good and now you're ruining it. You and the goddamn Sarsenis," he said bitterly.

I turned to him shaking my head as slowly as an old sage. "It's not me, it's not the Sarsenis, it's not the man in the moon," I said, my heart cracking with sadness. "It's you. It's you. It's you." Then I turned and walked to the door.

"Where do you think you're going?" he said to my back.

"Out of here."

He sprinted to the door. "No you're not," he said, blocking me.

"Get out of my way."

He opened his mouth and laughed at me.

I folded my arms. "Okay, Ben. But you can't stand there forever. And I'm telling you right now, I'm telling you if you go through with these—murders—I'll never sleep with you again."

He thrust his face at me, moving it close, smiling a kind of non-smile, his skin the color of copper. I reached around him for the doorknob but he stopped me with one thick manicured hand. Then he grabbed a fistful of my robe at the neck and without taking his eyes off my face, ripped it off, letting it drop to the floor. As I reached for it, he pushed me against the wall and ripped off my chemise. Naked, I ran to the bathroom, but he caught my arm and pulled me over to the rumpled bed. I grabbed the bedpost. He yanked my arm away. "Stop it!" I screamed, clutching it with my other hand. He put both his arms around my waist and tossed me on the bed as if I were a rag doll. I scrambled to my feet. He grabbed my hair, pulled me back down on the bed, and got on top of me. His face was red, wild-eyed, moist with sweat; his mouth open and oddly twisted. I saw the little black hairs in his nostrils. I saw the pores on his nose. I twisted and rolled my body from side to side but he pinned my hips to the bed. I beat him with my fists. He hit me hard across the face and jammed his tongue in my mouth. It felt like a wet rag. I bit it and he hit me again, harder, this time on my shoulder. I raised my knee aiming for his bulging crotch but he grabbed it, spread my legs, held my wrists over my head, and entered my pinned-down, spread-eagled body. I screamed. He held his big hand over my mouth and began his hard, dry, hot thrusting. I tried to bite his finger but his hand gripped my mouth shut. The raw shoving kept on, burning. Tears slid into my ears. My nose was running and I couldn't breathe. He didn't stop. I was afraid he would never stop. Then he abruptly cried out and emitted a massive moan. Rolling off me, he lay collapsed and breathless on his back in his monogrammed blue silk pajamas. I gasped for air. The smell of sweat and semen made me gag. He turned over, and I pulled myself off the bed and stumbled from the room, trying to cover my naked body with my torn robe. Feeling semen snake down my thigh like a sticky finger, I climbed the steps to the attic on rubbery legs and banged on Francine's door. The room was quiet. I beat the door with my fists. When Francine opened it, my knees collapsed.

"Mrs. Gold!! Lordy, Lordy," she said, catching me. She led me slowly to the bed. Shivering, I lowered my raw body into it. Francine removed the torn robe from my fist, finger by finger and covered me with a blanket. Then she wiped my wet face with a towel.

"Francine—"

"Shh, don't talk."

"Francine, I—"

"Mrs. Gold, ain't no need to say nothin'."

I watched her take a bottle from the closet and fill a shot glass. "Drink," she ordered, holding the brandy to my mouth.

I emptied the glass and Francine filled it again. Then she handed me two aspirins.

"Lock the door," I whispered

"I did already."

Shivering again, my opened body an aching wound, I lowered my head to the pillow. "Do you have another blanket?"

Francine pulled the olive green army blanket down from the shelf in her closet and covered me.

"Francine?"

"Yes, Mrs. Gold."

"Stay here with me?"

"I'll stay. Try to rest now. Try to sleep."

I closed my eyes. I heard a peculiar sound, like a cat whimpering.

"Shh, Mrs. Gold, quiet yourself. You all right, shh."

So that weird whine had been coming from my own mouth.

"That's better; try to rest now," Francine said, blotting my soaked face.

She sat down on the edge of the bed and clinging to her hand, I began to feel the brandy dissolve my sore body into the soft mattress and warm blankets, heating my chest, numbing my bruises, weighing down my eyes. Through heavy lids, I watched Francine settle into her chair. Francine was here. The door was locked. I slept.

* * *

It was dark in the room when I woke. I heard a clock ticking somewhere and groped for a bedside lamp. Seven o'clock. I had slept all day. Francine was gone. The lamp cast long shadows on the slanted ceiling and Francine's prim room. There were two small windows under the dormers covered with white chintz curtains, a lounge chair and lamp, a chest of drawers, a radio, a copy of *Readers Digest*. A simple room for an uncomplicated life. I thought of the silks and brocades downstairs, felt my shoulder ache as I tried to get out of bed, and wanted to trade lives.

Moving carefully, trying not to jar my gnawing head and pounding shoulder, I made it to the bathroom. In the mirror over the sink I saw the black and blue bruise just under my left eye, and another that fanned my left shoulder like a dark moth. I got into the shower and stood there a long time, trying not to think, soaking up the steam, letting the hot water massage my raw shoulder, washing, washing, as if the heat could restore my invaded body. I washed until the water turned cold.

I crawled back into bed and in a moment Francine came into the room with a tray full of food and one of my robes. "I heard the shower," she said, moving briskly. "You lookin' better. How you feelin'?"

"Hungry," I said, eying the food, now aware that I hadn't eaten in twenty-four hours. Francine helped me get the robe on over my sore shoulder and I sat up in bed with the tray on my lap, and chewing on the right side of my mouth, finished off the lamb chops, green beans, baked potato, lettuce and tomato salad, while Francine sat in the chair and leafed through the *Readers Digest*. When I finished, Francine poured a cup of tea for me from a flowered china teapot. I felt better. It surprised me.

"Is my husband home?"

"Yes, ma'am."

"Is Bobby—Mr. Keane—here?"

"He done been and gone," she said picking the tray up from my lap and starting for the door.

"Francine? Would you bring me some clothes from my room? I don't want to go in there."

She nodded without looking at me.

"And, Francine. Thanks. Thanks for helping me."

"You ain't the first I seen like that," Francine said dryly. "I'll get some beefsteak for them bruises.

* * *

An hour later, dressed in the gray wool dress that Ben had bought me on one of our New York trips, my hair combed and the dark bruise on my eye subdued by powder to a pale mauve, my shoulder throbbing, I came down the narrow attic steps and almost bumped into Ben.

"Kate," he said, "I've been waiting for you all day."

I tried to go around him, but he blocked my path. I was afraid I would start screaming.

"I just want to say I'm sorry."

"Get out of my way."

"Please. Let me talk to you."

"So talk."

"Not here," he said, taking my arm.

I jerked it away, sending a sharp pain through my shoulder. "Don't touch me."

"Let's go down to my office."

Now I was allowed into his secret world. Was the rape my initiation? Ben watched me intently as I stood there wondering what to do. But his invitation to the sanctum sanctorum was irresistible, and I preceded him down the steps.

Ben's and Bobby's windowless, wood-paneled offices opened off the reception room. There were two armchairs in Ben's office and a wide desk cluttered with papers. The coffee table held several copies of the *Saturday Evening Post*, *Colliers* and *Time* magazines, and the morning edition of the *Cleveland Plain Dealer*. There was a large photograph of me in a silver frame on his desk. It could have been a doctor's office.

"Please sit down," he said, politely, closing the door.

"Leave the door open," I said.

He obediently opened it.

He cleared his throat and looked at me. "Does that—does that bruise—bother you?"

I stared at him. "No."

He cleared his throat again. "But are you—" he stopped. "Kate, are you all right?"

I looked at him steadily.

He sat down, sighing. "Okay, I don't blame you for being mad. I just want you to know—" he stopped and cleared his throat again. "I want to tell you I'm sorry. Very."

"You told me," I said, starting to leave the room.

"I love you, Kate," he said to my back.

"You've got a strange way of showing it."

"I have a temper—"

"So I noticed."

"After this morning—" he stopped. "After what happened, I don't have the right to expect anything from you. I'm just begging you to listen so I can apologize, so I can talk to you," he said earnestly in a gentle voice, his mouth in a tentative smile. "Please, Kate, sit down. Just for a minute."

Knowing full well of his velvety, treacherous charm, I surprised myself and sat down. I watched him take a bottle of Canadian Club from a drawer in his desk. "Do you want a drink?" he asked.

"No."

"Mind if I have one?"

"I don't care what you do."

He half filled a glass and took it with him to the chair behind his cluttered desk. The dim office was lit by a lone lamp on his desk and smelled of the basement's moldy dampness. "You know, Kate," he said, "most of the guys in this business don't tell their families anything about what they do. Sure, the wives know something's going on, but they like all the luxuries. They like being well-provided for, you know, and they either don't want to know or don't care." He looked down into his glass. "You used to be like that, too." He looked up and gave me a weak grin. "But you changed on me."

"You're a liar. You lied to me from the beginning."

"I was afraid I'd lose you if you knew, that you wouldn't marry me."

I gazed at the wall over his head. I didn't want to think about that. For all I knew I would have married him anyway. Didn't Vivian try to warn me?

"You're so quiet," he said.

"I'm thinking about murder."

"Murder? Do you think I have an exclusive on murder? Isn't strapping some poor bastard in an electric chair murder? What about all the murdered kids in soldier suits? All dead bodies have the same stink. Murder's murder even if it's called something else."

"It's also been called wrong," I said, dryly. "And immoral."

"Immoral? Morality's Friday night in temple," he said bitterly. "Morality's lip service in church. That's where you'll find morality."

I pulled myself to my feet.

He looked up at me from his chair. "Kate, let me educate you in the ways of the real world. I'd be out of business overnight if there weren't politicians, cops, judges—not to mention all my law-abiding customers in it with me right up to their asses. I'm only one link in a very long chain of fine, upstanding citizens." He paused. "And don't look at me like that. Your society and mine is exactly the same, except yours is a hypocrite."

I stood there, feeling the dampness of the basement chilling my bones. My shoulder pulsed. The sky from Francine's window had been a crisp navy blue studded with stars and I wanted to see it again; I wanted to go upstairs and make a cup of hot tea; I wanted to breathe the benign kitchen smells of ordinary lives; I wanted to be anywhere but here arguing murder and hypocrisy with Ben Gold. I headed for the door.

"I love you," Ben said again.

I turned and sat back down. "Enough to get out of this business?"

"Look. You're completely apart from all that. Love has nothing to do with it."

"Then what does?" Suddenly I wanted to know about this stranger I found myself married to. Who charms and repels me. Plots murders and adores children. Rapes and loves music. And *me*. Says he loves me.

"Talk to me, Ben."

"What about?"

"Well, you've never told me anything about yourself—it's as if I'm a stranger."

He was silent so long, holding his drink and staring at the floor, I thought he hadn't heard me. Then he said, "I watched a little, skinny, sweet man shrivel up and die a terrible death, a slow death, an hour at a time."

"Of cancer?"

"Of cancer of the heart. Of grief. Of fear. Of shame. Of having no control over his own goddamn life."

"Your father."

"Yeah. My old man. I think I knew I didn't want to be like him before I could walk."

"What about your mother?"

"My mother? You met my mother."

I tried to imagine Ben as a baby, lying small and helpless in a crib, or later riding a bike, playing baseball on the corner lot, coming home from school in his cap and knickers, swinging his books on a strap. He seemed to have got here without parents, sprung whole and exotic from the earth or sky, full blown, like a god or the devil, always as smooth and arrogant as now, his body humming with power. I knew this was nonsense; of course, I knew that Ben was a mortal man like any other, but this had no effect on the way his presence could stir both my vigilance and excitement, even now, even as he sat quietly slumped in his chair.

"Did you grow up in Cleveland?"

"No, Detroit. We left when I was fourteen," he said. "My father worked on the assembly line at Ford and Henry Ford hated Jews so much he fired my old man just because he wouldn't work on the

Sabbath. I had a kid's daydream of killing the bastard when I got big enough. I even had a plan." Ben put his elbows on his desk and leaned forward. "See, I knew Ford would make a perfect target because he went out in the woods bird-watching, and I was a pretty good shot, even then. Anyway, the leader of the gang I was running with got sent up and my old man pulled me off the streets. He sold the copper samovar he'd brought over from Russia for two bus tickets to Cleveland and we squeezed into his sister's three-room apartment. My aunt and uncle and their two kids had the bedroom, my father slept on the in-a-door bed in the living room, and I had a cot in the kitchen." He drained his glass and sat holding it. "The only difference between Detroit and Cleveland was my old man didn't have his samovar anymore." He stared down into his empty glass. "I gave him money and he threw it down the toilet. I'd bring food home and he dumped it in the garbage. My uncle worked in a kosher butcher shop, but my father never found a job. He just sat with his prayer shawl and yarmulke, read the Torah, and dovened and dovened and sort of faded away. I moved out. I left him to his prayers. He died. He was thirty-nine years old." Ben got up and refilled his glass. "I've never told this to anyone before," he mumbled.

That's what Bobby told me last night. I've never told this to anyone, he said. Am I supposed to be honored or something by their dirty little secrets? I wished they'd kept their true confessions to themselves. I wished I'd never laid eyes on either one of them.

"You know something?" he was saying. "I'm glad you know this stuff—I actually feel sort of relieved. And if you find it in your heart to forgive me for the lies—and for—for—this morning—maybe we can put this behind us. Maybe we can start over."

I got up.

"Kate, I asked you to forgive me. I don't know what else I can do."

"You can call off the murders."

He looked up at me from his desk and seemed to become vulnerable under my stare. Standing over him, aware of my advantage, I allowed the room to fill with silence. Ben slid down into the chair and stretched his legs ahead. He sat up and ran his fingers through his hair. Then he said, sighing, "Let me think it over."

"When will you decide?"

"Soon. It'll have to be soon."

"Tomorrow?"

"Yes. Tomorrow."

I nodded. It was the best I could get out of him.

He got up, kissed me lightly on the cheek, and opened the door for me. As I climbed the stairs to the guest room I realized my shoulder had stopped throbbing. Hope was better than beefsteak.

Chapter 13

The next morning Ben wasn't anywhere in the house. The newspaper was on the breakfast room table so he had already been to Jake's newsstand. Don't worry, I told myself, sitting down at the breakfast table. He just went somewhere on an early errand.

"Coffee, Mrs. Gold?"

I looked up at Francine holding the percolator and nodded. I tasted the eggs in front of me and put the fork down. I couldn't eat. Something I couldn't name was drifting around the edges of my mind. It was too quiet. Something's wrong. My nerves stretched, vibrating like hot wires; I could feel the pulse of the house, smell sour odors from the garbage can, hear a single droning insect.

I got up, opened the front door, and looked up and down the street. There was no sign of Ben; only early faint sunlight, dusty budding trees. Everything looked ordinary, harmless. Innocent. The Marconi's house across the street had the same For-Sale sign, Mr. Prose next door backed his car out of the driveway just as he did every morning at eight, and blonde Amy Whitman opened her front door in a red robe and picked up her newspaper. A green Pontiac drove past, then a blue Ford, people on their way to work or a morning errand, men and women leading normal, safe lives. Folks who would die in bed of old age. Folks who thought murder only happened in James Cagney movies and newspaper headlines. People I understood.

Nothing's wrong, I told myself, sitting down again at the breakfast table. Just nerves. Ben could have changed his mind about the murders—didn't he say he'd think it over? Didn't he say he loved me? Didn't he say he wanted to put this behind us and start over?

I tried again to eat the eggs and suddenly, fork in midair, I knew what it was. I knew what was wrong. The morning newspaper was in its usual place on the table, but from the edge of my vision I saw that the front page was missing.

I leafed through it. "Francine!" I yelled. "Have you seen the front page?"

"No, ma'am," she called from upstairs.

I looked again, slowly this time, carefully turning each page one at a time. It wasn't there. Leaving the paper scattered over the table, I grabbed my coat and ran through the alley near our house to the newsstand. But *The Cleveland Plain Dealer* was sold out leaving only the *Readers Digest, Ladies Home Journal*, and a bunch of other magazines on its shelves. Pearson's drug store was six blocks away and the car was gone, but even if it had been there I didn't know how to drive it.

Chased by dread, feeling the cold air inside my nostrils, watching my breath push out in smoky spurts, I ran. With fear in my legs, I ran. I ran past Amy Whitman's Georgian, past the Utterback's Cape Cod, past the house of the widower Mr. Boehm and the Rev. Klostermeyer's and the Danford's. I ran watching my flying feet. I ran with my coat flapping behind me. I ran across streets without stopping. I ran past a startled lady pushing a buggy. I almost ran into the milkman and his rack of bottles who appeared in my path as suddenly as an apparition. I ran soundlessly as if I were dreaming. When I finally arrived at the familiar little neighborhood drug store, I was surprised, as if I had expected to wake up in my bed.

Panting, my cold body sweating, I opened the door. But the newspapers were not in their usual place at the front window. I ran to the back where Mr. Pearson was unpacking a carton of toothpaste.

"Where's the *Plain Dealer*?" I asked in a pitiful thread of a voice. He nodded to the side of the store at the pile of newspapers as high as my knee. I walked slowly, as slowly as I could, passing Mrs. Pearson behind the cash register. I saw the headline on the front page before I got there:

BROTHERS FOUND MURDERED IN LOCKED CAR

I picked up the newspaper:

Cleveland, Ohio, April 12.

> **The bodies of Mario and Salvatore Sarseni were discovered at 2 AM today by Officer John Reilly when he investigated a black late-model Studebaker that appeared to be stalled at a traffic light at 96th St. and Euclid Ave.**
> **Both men had been shot in the side of the head several times with a tommy gun. Mario Sarseni, 25, was found slumped over the steering wheel and the body of Salvatore Sarseni, 23, was in the passenger**

seat. Officer Reilly reported that there was a great deal of blood pooled on the floor. Both doors were locked from the inside.

The bodies were taken to the city morgue where they were identified by family members. Judging by the bullet-shattered windows, the direction of the bullets, and the position of the bodies police theorize they were shot through the closed windows by at least two gunmen, one on each side of the car, as the Sarseni brothers waited for the traffic light to change. Police have impounded the automobile and are interviewing the Sarsenis' family and friends for clues to the identity of the killers.

Mario and Salvatore Sarseni, whose family own the Sarseni Fruit & Vegetable Market on Scovil Ave., were believed to be involved in bootlegging operations.

It was an ordinary morning newspaper in my trembling hand, the same *Plain Dealer* I had read hundreds of times, now turning a husband into the murderer of two black sheep sons, twenty-three and twenty-five, respectively, their parents crying and crossing themselves in a tiny living room. Suddenly, ancient murders, centuries of murders, weeping mothers of the ages, all seemed to be embodied in Ben Gold. I thought I was going to be sick on the newspaper.

My heart shriveled with shame. How could I have known about the approaching murders of two human beings and not prevented them? I had been too weak, too frightened, too foolish. I was an accomplice because I sat in on the murder plot and did nothing. My myth of innocence—of my husband's and now mine—was shattered. He had me now. I knew too much. Ben would never let me go and I would not be able to bear his presence. I cursed my nosiness, my demand for information. I wished I could wind my life back to the beginning, like a film. I wished I could start it all over. But I knew I could not. Nothing, *nothing*, could be retrieved.

I sat down on a stool at the soda fountain and my mother oddly materialized, bowing her head. I obediently prayed for the Sarsenis' souls and my own salvation for the murderer's penetration of my excited, yielding body. But when I looked up there was no sign from heaven of either forgiveness or damnation—only a cardboard Coca Cola girl in her yellow bathing suit and yellow hair, holding her Coca Cola bottle in smiling triumph over her perfect knees. I longed for her cardboard innocence and my own despised past.

Mr. Pearson handed me a tissue from the Kleenex box he kept behind the counter and I realized tears were running down my cheeks. "You'd better let me give you something for that black eye," he said.

Just then the door of the small drug store burst opened so suddenly Mr. Pearson wheeled around. But even staring up into Coca Cola land, I knew who it was.

Seconds later Sam said in my ear, "Ben wants you home." He gripped my arm, nodded to Mr. Pearson, and led me firmly off the stool and out the door.

"How did you know where I was?" I asked, when we were in the car.

"Ben figured it out," Sam said, steering the Packard away from the curb. "He figured you went out to get a paper."

"Because the front page just happened to be missing?"

"So if you know something's going on why did you do such a stupid thing like go out by yourself?"

I touched the window. "Is this bullet-proof?"

"You bet your sweet life."

"Why wasn't the Sarsenis'?"

"How the hell do I know? Lucky it wasn't."

"Unlucky for them."

He looked at me hard. "Whose side are you on?"

I watched the indifferent houses wistfully from the car's bulletproof window as we passed Mrs. Holloway on her knees in her azalea bed and the Whitman's maid walking from the bus. We were home in minutes. Sam parked in the driveway, dashed around the car, grabbed my arm, and hurried me to the front door in a half run. He banged on the door three times, stopped and knocked twice. The door opened. Although a glaring sun shone outside, the living room was as dark as a moonless midnight. As my eyes adjusted, I made out Ben and Bobby lit by fringed lamps bearing dim circles of light. I had lived in that house over a year and never noticed the heavy brown curtains covering the windows that had been concealed behind the golden draperies, waiting only for a murder or two and a pull on a silken rope.

"Thank God," Bobby said when he saw me. His eyes widened. "Where'd you get the shiner?"

"We were very worried about you," Ben said, coming over to me.

I backed away. "Liar!"

Ben glanced at Bobby who was staring at the seascape on the wall with his hands in his pockets. "We'll talk later," he said, turning to Sam who had been watching with interest. "Go hit the mattress, Sam. If you need to reach me, ring once, hang up, and I'll call you from a pay phone."

Bobby was putting on his coat.

"Where do you think you're going?" Ben asked him.

"We're hiding out," Bobby said, "I'd just as soon be home. We're out of business anyway 'til the heat's off."

"The hell we are. I want you here."

"What for? We can't go out, we can't use the phone—"

"There's still pay phones."

"Sure, while we get our heads blown off."

"Christ, Bobby, stop talking like an old woman. I got the Packard fixed up like a tank. Nobody can touch us."

"Except when we get out to use the phone."

"We keep each other covered."

"I thought Sam was taking the car," Bobby said.

"No, Sam hides out in the rented room. He doesn't need it. You take him and bring the car back—we've got a business to run here. You have a couch in your office, there's a bathroom down there, and you're here 'til the heat's off."

"And when will that be?"

"Maybe soon."

"What's soon?"

Ben shrugged. "A few weeks give or take, maybe a month. I sent word to the Sarseni boys they have a job with us for two-fifty a week which is more than they ever made in their lives."

"What makes you think they'll take it? What makes you think they won't come after us?"

"Because the money's good and it's better for their health," Ben said, looking flushed, exhilarated. "But you never know. So we hide out."

"Ben you could've started a whole damn war—"

"Bobby, stop bellyaching already. Legs's dead, Capone's in jail—"

"What about the police?" I asked.

Ben, Bobby, and Sam all turned and stared at me as if they had forgotten I was standing there. "Don't worry about it," Ben said, turning away.

"Let's go, Sam," Bobby said, pulling on his coat.

"Bobby!" I cried.

He stopped at the door.

"Be careful," I said.

He nodded without looking at me and left, followed by Sam.

Ben bolted the door behind them and walked toward me. "It was very foolish of you going out alone like that."

I backed away and turned my head as if he had a stench.

"I didn't want you to read about it in the paper like that," he said. "I wanted a chance to explain—"

"Explain what? That you're a liar?" I was still standing in the middle of the living room in my coat, like a visitor. Which I passionately wished I was.

"Kate, I didn't lie. Honest to God I tried to stop Sam, but it was too late—he'd already left."

Rooted to the floor, I closed my eyes and imagined myself opening the front door and running, the wind pushing through my clothes, pulling my hair back, my feet flying, getting away, getting somewhere else, anywhere but here.

I left the room. Holding the banister, I climbed the stairs slowly, laboriously, one step at a time. Upstairs, the guest room windows were curtained with more of that heavy brown fabric and I had to feel for the light switch. When was this room murder-proofed? Why hadn't I noticed? How many murders before the Sarsenis? How many to come?

"Get away from the window," Ben said behind me.

I backed away and faced him.

"Get out!" I shouted.

He sat down on the arm of the easy chair. "Kate," he said, wearily, "I told you. I tried to stop Sam. I called all over town. I went out looking for him—"

"For God's sake, Ben, we can all be killed!"

His face colored. "You think I can't protect you? Is that what you think? I assure you no one's harming a hair on the head of Ben Gold's wife."

"So now we have to live in the dark," I said. "We have to hide from the Sarseni gang. From the police. From God knows who else. Who else Ben? What other dirty little surprises have you got for me? You know something? I'm sick of your damn secrets and your lies and I'm sick to death of you. So do me a big favor and get out of here."

Ben stood up. "Kate," he said, "I've been thinking about last night—about what you said about quitting. And you know what? I decided you were absolutely right," he said earnestly.

I groaned. "Do tell."

"The only thing is, after the heat's off I have to make a deal with someone—the Sarseni boys or someone—you can understand that—I've got trucks, cases of booze, payrolls, drivers, things to wind up—it takes a little time, okay? But I'm getting out. You can count on it." He sat down again and looked up at me wistfully. "I'm not exactly stupid, you know. I want to live long enough to have babies, to have you and our children and a family."

"Such reason. Such logic. All of a sudden."

"My temper," he said, getting up again. "My terrible, miserable, unfortunate temper. It's gotten me in trouble my whole life." He put his hands on my shoulders and gazed into my eyes. "Please believe me,

Kate. I'm quitting the business. I swear. I swear on the lives of our unborn children."

I didn't know whether to believe him or not—the question was moot, academic, irrelevant. I felt lost somewhere in Ben's rot, a gangster's wife in this fancy brown-curtained prison, hiding from shadow assassins bent on retaliation, my exhilarating moments of resolve of only hours ago, dead; vaporized by Ben's smiles, lies, and blight.

Chapter 14

Hiding out, our lives slipped into a routine. Outside, the front and back yards had been stripped of their shrubbery, lights installed, and two sentries suddenly appeared dressed like gardeners. But inside, Ben and Bobby worked in their offices as usual while I reread everything in the house and wrote in my journal, while Francine turned out meals from the basement pantry that had suddenly been stocked with enough canned and packaged food to feed an army.

During dinner on the third or fourth evening, there was a sudden knock on the door. A gun materialized in Ben's hand like a magician's scarf as Bobby motioned to Francine and me to crawl under the table. Ben moved swiftly on his elbows and knees to the living room window. Rising, he flattened himself against the wall, lifted the edge of the drape, and peered out. Then he put the gun in his shoulder holster, and opened the front door.

Francine, Bobby, and I crept out from under the dining room table, not looking at each other. Francine disappeared into the kitchen, Bobby brushed off his pants and sat down at his place, and I straightened my dress and stood staring at Bobby calmly eating macaroni and cheese while Francine's eggbeater whirred away in the kitchen. The dining room of the American gangster by Norman Rockwell—next week's *Saturday Evening Post* cover. Well, why not? Francine was whipping Jell-O in the kitchen, Bobby was putting butter on his roll, my husband was speaking warmly to the two policemen at our door. Suddenly afraid I would start laughing hysterically, I stuffed a roll in my mouth.

"It's good to see you boys," Ben was saying at the door. "How's that young son of yours, Tom?"

"Doin' just fine, Ben. Finally sleepin' through the night."

"Well, I guess Laura's happy about that."

"Yes, sir, that boy was wearin' her out."

"Well," Ben said, "that's the way it goes. Can I offer you boys a cup of coffee?"

"No thanks." There was silence and then the sound of throat clearings. "Say, Ben, I hate to intrude here at dinner time like this;

please excuse this intrusion here, but we're gettin' complaints over at headquarters from your neighbors—the Prose's called two, three times."

"What's their problem?"

"Well, they saw the gardeners standing around, the bushes gone and all, those bright lights, and they wondered. It's none of their business, of course. It's your home, but you understand when two, three neighbors call up, Jack here and me, we got to show up."

"Tom," Ben said, solemnly, "it's your job."

"So what should I tell 'em?"

"Tell them we had to dig up the yard looking for a big leak in the basement."

"Okay, yeah, I'll tell them that. Thanks, Ben. Sorry to bother you."

"No bother at all. It's always good to see you boys. Give our regards to Laura."

"Sweeten Tom's next envelope," Ben said to Bobby as he sat down at the table. Bobby nodded and took another roll from the breadbasket while Ben dug into the food on his plate. His suit was still mussed from his floor-crawl, and he looked different to me, older and heavy-featured. Unfamiliar. I watched his mouth open to forkfuls of macaroni and cheese, smelled its thick odor as the platter passed back and forth, heard their voices in a hum as if they were in another room. My chair faced the living room and when I looked up, the white baby grand piano that no one could play, the golden cupid lamps with their shimmering fringe, and the gilt-framed velvet couch suddenly took on the look of an expensive bordello.

"Excuse me," I said, getting up.

"You okay?" Ben asked.

But I was on my way upstairs. I had to get away from there.

* * *

The days slipped by one after the other while my heart jumped at sounds, closed with boredom; I felt it stop and then pound and then capsize—I was afraid I would go crazy. My fury at Ben and turmoil over Bobby exhausted me, exhilarated me, tormented me. I did not know how to read anymore, or how to think, or what to do with the tangle of fear and tedium and despair that I felt.

Each lamp-lit twenty-four hours behind the covered windows was the same, without even the rhythm of daylight and evening to mark the passing of time. I tried to count the days in their perpetual night and grotesquely banal routine, but I lost track and after a while it didn't matter.

Pacing the living room one afternoon, trying not to jump out of my skin, I became aware of friendly cooking sounds and aromas drifting out of the kitchen, and of Francine's serene presence.

"Something smells good," I said, walking into the kitchen. "What's for dinner?"

"Tomato soup, salmon patties, baked potatoes, apple pie."

"Can I help?" I asked, taking deep breaths, trying to become as composed as Francine.

She didn't look up from the piecrust she was rolling out. "No thanks."

"Please, Francine, let me."

"Everything's done made already."

"Would you let me make dinner one of these days? Would you do that for me?" I asked, my voice breaking with longing for the rituals of normal lives.

"You know how to cook?"

"Since I'm ten."

"I been cookin' since I'm ten too, but I'm a good bit older than you. That's a long time to cook."

"You're doing a good job with those cans."

"I try my best," she said, pressing the crust into the pie plate.

I leaned against the counter and looked at her. "Francine, does this upset you? Living like this?"

She glanced at me. "No, ma'am, it don't upset me."

"Even though you can't go out, even though it may be—it could be—dangerous?"

"Listen, most folks is out of work. Some is hungry. And them that do have jobs don't get paid because the boss's broke too. Mr. Gold pays me every single Saturday and he pays me good." She dusted the flour off her hands. "I been with him a long time, and what he do for a livin' ain't none of my business and ain't nobody's business." Moving with an elegant efficiency, she walked back to the sink and washed the mixing bowl briskly. "You know what my sister make crocheting hats in New York City? Eighty cent a week." Drying her hands on a towel, she looked at me, the whites of her eyes tinged with pink, her skin as luminous and smooth as brown satin. "Her daughter, she get two and a half cent to make a apron—that's twenty cent a day. But what can they do? Her husband been out of work so long he stuff newspapers in his shoes." She turned away and I watched silently while she peeled and sliced apples with her small, quick hands and layered them in the piecrust. "You know what my sister's husband do to eat? When he out looking for work, he order a cup of coffee at a diner for a nickel. Then after he drink it he axe for hot water in his cup and then he mix it with the ketchup on the table. That what he do to eat." She slid the pie into the oven and turned back to me. "I got me a job. Mr. Gold treat me fine. I eat good. I can help my sister and my daughter and put away for my old age. And I thank the good Lord." She folded her arms and gazed at me. "Am I upset? No, ma'am, my mama didn't raise no silly girl."

And don't you be no silly girl either, I told myself, picking up a potato to peel. Francine's right. If it weren't for Ben I'd be working some miserable job. If I could find one. Living with my mother. Maybe standing in a soup line. Okay, Ben's made some mistakes in the past, serious mistakes. I know that. I understand that. But he said he's leaving the business. He swore. When all this is over, when we're not hiding out, everything'll change. Everything'll be okay.

I dried my hands and went upstairs trying to calm down and count my blessings.

* * *

I think it was about two weeks later at the dinner table that Ben said, "I've got some news. The guys from the Sarseni gang all start work for me tomorrow."

"Good," Bobby said. "Now I can go home."

"Whoa, wait a minute," Ben said. "Not yet. I have to watch these guys—especially Vinnie—get reports from the boys. When it looks like they're all okay, you go home. Not before."

"So how long?" Bobby asked.

"Like I said, we go one step at a time."

"Ballpark."

Ben shrugged. "A couple more weeks, maybe longer." He put his fork down and took my hand in both of his. "Don't look so sad, honey. I know this is hard for you. I know you're disappointed that we have a while to go in this situation. But I'll make it up to you, and that's a promise. You'll see."

But I wasn't thinking about this "situation" as Ben so delicately put it. I was thinking about Bobby. Our closeted hothouse existence seemed to create a lush environment that made my yearning for him grow denser, and with each day of our confinement he was more and more on my mind. I could see Bobby at the edge of my vision, and glancing at his pale face and calm eyes that showed nothing, that refused even to look at me, I felt tears spring to my eyes.

"Aw, Kate," Ben said, looking at me, "don't cry. I'll wind things up as soon as I can."

I looked down at the tuna patties. I wanted never to see tuna fish again in any of its disguises—croquettes, patties, casseroles topped with corn flakes, sandwiches with mayonnaise. I wanted fresh lettuce. I wanted to bite into an apple. I wanted to see the sky. I wanted to feel Bobby's arms around me. I wanted to go back to the time before I ever laid eyes on Ben Gold.

"Francine," Ben called," is there any of that spice cake left?" He turned to Bobby and me. "I called this whole operation right on the nose, didn't I, folks? Things are working out okay. Soon as all this settles down we'll take a trip with Sam—okay you two? We'll have a celebration in New York, like before," he said, beaming at us with his wonderful smile.

* * *

The days dragged on, each one exactly the same, everyone growing listless, speaking less, moving less, as if malnourished into a scurvy of the spirit by the airless rooms and covered windows and perennial night. I began to feel that our release would never come, as if Francine in the kitchen, Ben and Bobby in their offices, me drifting from room to room, were all eternally trapped until, without growing old or dying, we would all turn into smoky ghosts, fleshless and damned.

We celebrated Passover with two half-burned yellow candles Francine dug up, a bottle of Manechevitz wine that Ben produced, and a dinner of noodles and canned salmon, canned tomatoes, and rolls. But neither the candles or the wine could do much for our dismal little celebration. When we finally finished the wedges of German chocolate cake and coffee, the three of us backed our chairs away from the table and scattered; I went to the living room for the radio's NBC concert, and Ben and Bobby returned to the basement.

And then, a week later when I came downstairs, the brown draperies were gone and Ben was standing in the sunny room looking out the exposed window, his black hair shining in the sun's glare.

"All clear, Kate," he said, turning to me and smiling. Heart racing, I ran to the window and squinted at the brilliant, liberated sky.

"The sun makes your hair like a flame," Ben said, putting his arm around me.

I smiled at him. "Let's go outside!"

"Naw, I just came in. You go ahead. I got work." He turned to Bobby who had joined us at the window. "Making Vinnie a boss turned out to be a good move. He's got the makings of a leader and he's keeping Fats and Izzy in line."

"I'll go outside with you," Bobby said to me. "Come on, Ben."

"Not me," Ben said. "I just came in."

My heart leapt as Bobby opened the door for me and we left the house. Alone. At last. Alone with Bobby. Even the guards had disappeared. Everything smelled fresh, new; it was one of those bright

April days vivid with sky and sun, and released into the innocent air with Bobby at my side, the wind pushing through my clothes; I thought my heart would burst.

"He knows," Bobby said, when we reached the sidewalk.

I stopped. "Knows what?"

"Keep on walking. He found out I made a deal for a building. He knows I'm quitting. He has ears everywhere. It was stupid of me not to tell him."

"Was he mad?"

Bobby shook his head. "He just asked me to put together a set of books and look for someone to replace me."

"But Ben's quitting, too. He promised me he'd quit," I said.

"If he's quitting why does he need someone to replace me?"

"He said he needs time to wind things up. But who knows? He's such a liar."

We had walked out of our neighborhood; the houses were smaller here, closer together; some had a chair or two pulled into the front yard for the spring morning. Daffodils and a few tulips were pushing up here and there in brave little gardens and red-cheeked children in jackets chased each other; one little boy got tangled up in our legs.

"So when are you leaving?" I asked, not looking at him.

"Depends how long it takes me to find someone Ben'll hire."

"Will I ever see you again?"

"I'm going to try to forget the Golds ever existed," he said.

I glanced at him. He wasn't kidding. "Well thanks," I said. "Thanks a lot. Me too?"

"You bet. Especially you. So don't invite me to dinner," he said, with some of his old banter. He took my arm. "We'd better get back to the house."

When we returned, Ben, Sam, and the Packard were gone and there was a note in the kitchen from Francine saying that she was visiting her daughter for the afternoon.

Bobby sat down on the couch. Pleased, thrilled, I sat down next to him.

"I'd better get down to my office," he said.

I wanted to hit him. I wanted to kiss him on the mouth. I wished he'd go. I wished he'd never leave my side.

"Why don't you just shove off," I said, standing up.

"What're you sore about?"

Sighing, I sat down again. My temper had a way of going as fast as it came. "I'm not sore, Bobby. It's just that—that—I hate to see you leave."

Bobby colored and looked so uncomfortable, I smiled and said,

"After all, you were best man at my wedding."

"Some wedding. You looked like a kid playing dress-up wobbling around in those high heels." He regarded me. "I felt sorry for you. Maybe it was the look on your face. Sort of too—I don't know—too somber or something. Too sad for a bride." He folded his arms. "But then I watched this sort of sad kid—you—grow up right before my eyes and become a woman, a real presence in this house." He gazed out of the window looking so remote and withdrawn I wanted to take his hand. But I didn't. I just said that he was the one looking sad.

He sighed. "I used to get rid of that feeling with money and women and cars—and, you know—excitement. Ben's excitement." He turned to me. "But it—the life—stopped doing it for me. I don't want that stuff anymore." He turned to the window and watched the sudden rain streaking down the glass. "I want to go back to college. I want a family, children. I didn't know I wanted all that until I knew you. Can you beat it? It took Ben's wife to show me I don't want Ben's life."

"But I thought you were leaving because of the murders."

"Red, I started to leave here a hundred times before the Sarsenis." He gazed at me for a long moment. "I didn't want to leave you when you wobbled up to the Justice of the Peace and I didn't want to leave you pregnant and I didn't want to leave you sweating and crying and ruining my car seat and I didn't want to leave you when Maggie died and I don't want to leave you now." He put his head down in his hands. "I have to go and fall in love with none other than Ben Gold's wife," he said miserably. "Of all the women in the entire goddamn world. I'm insane."

I thought that was about the weirdest declaration of love a woman ever heard, and it made me happier at that moment than I'd been in my entire life. I was breathless. "What did you say?" I panted.

"You heard me," he mumbled.

He loved me. He said he loved me. I didn't mean to cry, but there I was, weeping all over his sweater. He put his arms around me, or maybe it was me, maybe I put my arms around him. It just seemed to happen like the roll of the sea or the way you breathe. "Bobby, don't leave, stay. I can't bear it if you go. I love you," I said to his neck.

He started kissing me on my wet cheeks and all over my face with such love and tenderness that I had a feeling of sliding...sliding. We sank down on the couch pressing our bodies together and he kissed my mouth with his lips and his tongue and even—it seemed, his soul. His hand reached to my breast and his touch made me feel known in ways that Ben, with all his passion, never did and never could.

He jerked his hand back as if my breast was hot. "No," he said, sitting up, breathing. "It's impossible."

Trembling, I sat up slowly, straightening my clothes. "Not if I leave him. It's not impossible if I leave him."

"You can't leave him," he said flatly, loosening his tie. His face was red, moist. I could feel his heat. "If he'd kill two people before he gives up a truck and some whisky, what do you think he'd do if his wife left him?" Tucking in his shirt, he got up, walked over to the window, and stood there staring at the streaks of water sliding down the glass.

"Then don't leave. Stay here. Don't leave me."

He turned back to the window. "I'm leaving before I go crazy. And before I—we—start being stupid."

"Sure," I said, crying again. "Swell. You'll leave me behind with a—a—killer—a murderer—and go off to your nice new life. What about me? What am I going to do?"

He sat down on the couch and wiped my eyes with his handkerchief. Then he took my hand and kissed it, turned it over, and held my palm to his lips. I put my arms around him and held him close. He stroked my hair. We clung together and I didn't know if the tears on my face were Bobby's or mine.

Hearing the Packard in the driveway, we pulled apart. Bobby stood up, straightening his tie.

"Can't I see you again?" I whispered. "Before you leave?"

"Thursday, the same street corner. Nine o'clock." And he headed for the basement.

* * *

That night Ben wanted to go out to celebrate. And why not? The Sarsenis were obliterated, their gang was in his employ, the police were in his employ; after hiding in the dark we had emerged unscathed and triumphant into the shining spring sunshine. Who could blame him for wanting to commemorate such achievements? Who was more deserving?

So Ben and I went to Allie's. His buddies greeted us warmly with hugs, and after I obligingly toasted the occasion with champagne, feeling pleasantly unfocused, thinking of Thursday, of seeing Bobby on Thursday, thinking that he loved me, I drank champagne and then bourbon in coffee cups and danced the Charleston furiously with Ben, bumping into elbows and feet on the hot, crowded dance floor.

CHAPTER 15

I refused to believe Thursday would be the last time I'd see Bobby. We loved each other. And weren't we smart? I kept repeating this to myself until there was no room for doubt. Come on, Bobby, I'll say, it's a big world out there, we can put thousands of miles between us and a man as ignorant and smug as Ben. We can go to Europe. Brazil. Places Ben and his lapdog Sam have barely heard of. Bobby will put his arms around me and his eyes that are the blue of a child's crayon will shine, and he'll say, Red, honey, you're right; I was overreacting. We'll disappear and start a new life together. I felt the drama of our escape like a heroine in the movies. I was, after all, twenty years old.

But I began to notice things. Ben's cat eyes staring at me during dinner. Or was I imagining it? Did Ben see Bobby's hand linger on my neck when he helped me on with my coat yesterday? At night, in bed, Ben's lovemaking was different—rougher, quicker, hurting me.

I was getting worried. Were Bobby and I living in a stupid fantasy of escape? Stupidity would get us killed. Ben, I knew, was shrewd, lightning-quick, often lucky. If we pulled this off, we had to be better than he. Or we were done.

During lunch with Ben yesterday, heavy clouds dumped an unexpected spring snow, and as the wet flakes drifted down on the greening trees I was reminded of another life, of my father, young and slender, lifting my four-year-old self high on his shoulders to see the top of the Christmas tree; of squirming while he pulled and stretched my tangled hair into braids, my mother staring from the couch with empty, waxy eyes; of his smooth face in the shoe store looking gravely at the bones of my feet in Buster Brown's X- Ray machine. I walked proudly in my new stiff and tightly laced school shoes that day, my father holding my wrapped-up old shoes under his arm while we licked ice cream cones in Allen's Drug Store.

Now, I felt an unspeakable rage at my father for leaving me at a lunch table with a killer.

* * *

At last it was Thursday and Bobby. Francine had made pork chops, a specialty of hers, and I could get none of it past my throat. Not even the towering lemon meringue pie she made especially for me. I could only sit there helplessly and wait for Ben to finish his methodical eating. He had this ugly way of mopping up the gravy with his pork chop bone and licking it clean. Then in his own good time he'd always push away from the table, summon Sam, and leave.

But this time, after he asked for a second cup of coffee, he leisurely left the table, took the newspaper and stretched out on the couch.

I sat down, too. I didn't know what else to do. Bobby had said nine o'clock; there was still time. I took part of the newspaper from Ben and tried to read. I went into the kitchen to dry the dishes, but Francine sent me away. It was eight-thirty. Ben was still on the couch, his eyes closed.

I sat down again. At eight forty-five I said, "I think I'll visit my mother tonight."

His yellow eyes became alive. "Is that so," he said, looking at me like a prosecutor. "What's going on? You never visit her at night."

"Well," I said, wincing at his stare, "she's been working full time lately. And—you know—she isn't getting any younger—"

"I'll drop you off," he said, getting up.

"Okay," I said, alarmed. "I'll be just a few minutes."

"Doing what?"

"Changing. I don't want to wear my good dress to my mother's. And these high heels are killing me."

He looked at his watch. I held my breath. "Can't wait, gotta go. See you later," he said.

I kissed him. I really did. I said have a nice evening.

"Don't wait up," Ben said as he headed for the basement and Sam. I sat there until I heard the car door slam twice and the Packard back out of the driveway. It was ten minutes to nine. I made myself wait five more minutes. Then I called upstairs to Francine that I was going to visit my mother.

I waited fifteen minutes more, grabbed my coat, and left the house. It had been raining and the air smelled of the earth. I started running, the soft spring night brushing my face, the indifferent sky overhead beautiful with stars, the houses of benign lives casting faint beams of light into the dark night. I ran all the way to the street corner.

Bobby was waiting in the Pierce Arrow. I followed his instructions and slid down in the seat as we drove to his apartment.

I had long wondered where he lived when he was away from me, imagining a sort of bachelor's pad with women coming and going, making me sick with jealousy. I imagined booze in the ice box, maybe some beer, and little else. But remembering Ben's fringed lamps adorned with cupids, the satin and brocaded furniture, a white piano that no one could play, I half expected Bobby, long under Ben's influence, to have more of the same.

His apartment was some distance from Ben's Shaker Heights home, located in Shaker Square, a roundabout ringed with shops, a movie theater, restaurants, and a row of elegant apartment buildings adjacent to the Square. It took us over twenty minutes to get there and even slid down in my seat, I frequently sat up and looked over my shoulder for Ben's Packard. Finally arriving at Bobby's apartment, he parked and turned to me.

"Keep down in the seat," he said. "Wait five minutes, and then come inside to the elevator. My apartment is on the tenth floor—number ten sixteen. I've been watching and don't think we're being followed, but make sure before you leave the car."

I scanned the street, and stiff-necked from my uncomfortable position hiding in the Pierce Arrow, rode the elevator to 1016 along with a middle-aged, heavy-set man with a beard, who scared me. I knew well of Ben's diabolical resources.

But when Bobby opened the door, smiling, my fear evaporated. He put his arms around me, and I stayed in his embrace, wanting never to leave.

"Would you like something to eat or drink?" he asked, releasing me.

I looked around for the first time at the high-ceiling and oak-paneled walls and stuffed bookcases. "I want to see your apartment," I said.

Bobby gave me a tour. I had no idea what to expect. The rooms were stylish, sparsely but tastefully furnished. Unlike my idea of a bachelor's apartment, these rooms reflected a sense of order and design. And modernity; the apartment of a young gentleman. I shouldn't have been surprised at his surroundings, but I had seen Bobby for such a long time in Ben's moribund palace that it took me a few minutes to adjust. I wondered if Ben Gold had ever set foot in this place, with its Art Deco themes, and framed prints of paintings by Matisse and Picasso. Ben would know at once that he didn't belong here and would no-doubt be anxious to get on the elevator and ride back down to his tank-like Packard.

In the living room I noticed the inlaid wood on the furniture. Bobby escorted me to the kitchen, which I saw was barely used, yet spotless. Of course, the ice box was almost empty, but again, well tended. In the bathroom, the mirrors were polished with no spatters of toothpaste or shaving cream; the medicine cabinet was well organized and even contained such items as band-aids and iodine. Bobby's toothbrush looked new and hung from a small hook above the sink.

Whisky and beer was his business, but he offered tea and stale cookies. We sat, sipping, stunned by the fact of being alone together with our previous declarations of love still ringing in the air, and Ben's malignant, hovering presence between us. But later, in bed, the weight of Bobby's body, his darting erotic tongue, his rough cheek, his explosive entry into my secret virginal self, vanquished Ben completely, leaving us in a private singular and insulated world of our own making. We felt absurdly safe in our recklessness, as if our awakenings were so blessed by the gods that nothing bad could befall us.

In normal circumstances, perhaps we would not have felt this magical circle. But we believed it was there because we met night after night and were sure that Ben never knew. Our risk, our folly, seems incredible to me when I look back, but our youth and love swept us away, and I felt courage and strength pass back and forth through our bodies as if our combined selves created another, invulnerable identity. If we clung too desperately to each other and this illusion of invincibility, if we beat away the danger and our own recklessness, well, it only added to our fever.

The contrast between the apartment to which Bobby escaped after a tedious day doing calculations for a killer, and Ben's ornate bunker, unnerved and exhilarated me. In the days that followed my first visit, we went there nightly as soon as Ben and Sam left the house. Although Bobby and I had both discovered it was easier to get into Ben's life than out of it, we made our careful plans to escape—as thrilling as our lovemaking.

Chapter 16

Bobby waited at our street corner every night so tightly wound in our excitement I scarcely knew him from the careful Bobby of before. Impossibly handsome, his charm unleashed, he was as pale as a romantic poet and as touching as an awkward adolescent. His blue eyes burned, opening the world for me, for us; we were going to begin our lives together away from Ben. We were intoxicated with our urgency, our virtue.

Still, there was some of the cautious Bobby of before. One evening in his living room, he taught me how to use a gun. "Just in case," he said. He pulled on a pair of gloves, handed me another pair, saying, "Ben taught me to never touch a gun—not even to clean—without gloves."

The sight of the Smith & Wesson scared me. "Put on the gloves," he said, as I stood staring at the gun. I obediently put them on and watched him empty the pistol of its bullets. Then he stood behind me, took my hand and wrapped my fingers around its handle. His weight on my back, his breath on my neck, calmed me as he lifted my right hand and arm, turning me into a frightening stranger.

"Go ahead," he said, "keep your arm straight, point at the window, and pull the trigger. And remember, you've never shot before, so if you have to use it, be sure to get as close to the target as you can. Or you'll miss."

"But how? How can I get close?"

"Use your head. The gun has a silencer on it."

The trigger was tougher to pull than I thought it would be, but I squeezed hard with my index finger. The click made me jump.

He took the automatic from me, reloaded it, and put it into my handbag. My arm felt light and vulnerable without the weight of the gun; I missed the feeling it gave me of power. And yet I knew. I knew of the gun's danger and deadliness. The pistol in my handbag with its lipstick and wallet and comb and handkerchief had magically transformed me from a vulnerable 115-pound young girl into a dangerous adversary. At home, I hid it along side my book in the deep crown of my black hat in the closet. Awed and thrilled, I had a sweet dream that night of omnipotence. Of empowerment. Of rage.

* * *

Each night Bobby brought me back around eleven and I'd slip upstairs wondering if Francine believed that I had been to see my sick mother—my story to her when I left the house every night at eight-thirty. I thought Ben assumed I was home, as I had always been when he was out, and I just left it at that, managing to be in bed with Bobby's body and smell and love showered off.

Around Ben, I was tight, cheerful, afraid; at night with Bobby I was loose, moist with love, safe. Bobby stayed downstairs in his office during the day and I wrote him long flowery letters and composed embarrassing poems of love but was prudent enough not to carry out my plan of slipping them in his jacket pocket draped on the back of his office chair, or even of keeping them in my purse to give to him. Because I wasn't being ridiculously reckless, I thought I was being cautious

Since the Sarseni murders, Ben had earned a long-coveted and lucrative business connection with the Mafia, which was given to very few Jews. So full of himself about his elevated status as the now feared underworld boss, he went about his activities apparently oblivious of my transported state. My preoccupation, painted-on smile, listless response to sex, seemed not to make a dent in his attitude and awareness. Or did I imagine our life differently before Bobby entered it? Ben had his office hours, his meals with me, his nightly disappearances. He wound up his Victrola on Sunday nights, smiling and nodding to the scratchy arias. Once after sex he asked me if I had a headache. Another time he inquired about my mother's health. I told him she was very slowly improving. My replies must have satisfied him because he didn't bring the topics up again. It worried me. Later, I realized it was his diabolical scheming on his mind—hardly his lack of suspicion

Bobby and I knew Ben's habits. We made plans. The *Franconia* was sailing for Brazil in seventeen days. Although the *Carinthia* was leaving for England in four days, we'd then have to make our way around Africa to South America, adding almost two more months of travel—too much, we thought. (Of course, if we had taken the earlier *Carinthia* to England everything would have turned out differently. The irony haunted me for years.)

We decided that the night before the *Franconia* sailed, I would leave a note that I was going to my mother's for a day or two because she was ill. We would then take the night train to New York, taxi from

Grand Central to Pier 2, and board the *Franconia*. After a few days Ben would go to my mother's apartment, she would be bewildered or drunk or both, and Bobby and I would be on the high seas disguised as Geoffrey Foster and his younger brother Daniel, who was actually me dressed in Bobby's dead young brother's clothes, my hair piled up in a cap. Love had made us so cunning.

Chapter 17

My dearest,

Maybe because I have lived so long with lies—Ben's and my own—or maybe because of my love for you, or maybe the Catholic in me needs to confess, but it is very important to me that as we start our life together you know the truth about me and my connection to Ben. Also, as you read on, I think you'll understand that because of the remorse I feel it is easier for me to write than to tell you about the time before we met.

In the beginning, being with Ben felt like riding a roller coaster; exciting, scary and temporary, as if after the ride I could just climb off and get on with my real life.

When we talked in the car that night in the parking lot of the Marathon, I wanted your forgiveness and ducked any responsibility for being with Ben. But the truth is that even though I knew full well of his evil, he fascinated me. Or maybe it was the evil itself. I didn't know. What does anyone know at 18? I had enough of the arrogance of the young to think I could leave him any time I wanted. Wasn't I smarter? An accounting genius? Didn't I have a photographic memory? Even some college? Wasn't he just some tough guy from the streets who knew nothing? I could outwit Ben Gold. My plan was to accumulate enough money to go back to school. That was before I fell into Ben's life and my own lust.

So I wasn't the misled teenager I tried to show you. I wanted to stay with Ben because of his interest in me. Because of his weird authenticity—he was what he was. Because of his audacity. His rages that scared me and his charm that seduced me. The money he put in my pocket and the Pierce Arrow he put under me, that I loved like a kid with his first car. Which of course, I was. Young as he was, I looked up to him as the father I never had.

Ben had a girlfriend, a nurse at University Hospital, but until he met you women didn't interest him that much—a gun or knife was more exciting to him than sex. His lust was for murder. But for me—and I'm not proud of this—it was women. A natural blonde from Shaker Heights, a brunette waitress from my favorite restaurant, a girl in a skirt and sweater from Flora Stone Mather College, a violinist with the Cleveland Symphony. There were even a couple of married women I met at Allie's, that Ben, who happened to know their husbands, warned me off; either one would cheerfully put a bullet in my head and think nothing of it, he told me.

Then you arrived. And over time I became acutely aware of your bewilderment and confusion, and slowly saw, through your innocent eyes, that murder was a part of Ben's day, like going for his morning newspaper. It was as if your beauty and virtue and intelligence had been dropped from the sky by a benevolent God to show me the pathology of Ben's life. And mine. I saw, as if for the first time, that Ben's world corrupts the living, putting it in secret danger of contamination. Of Death.

When I used to go to Mass on Sunday with my mother, I walked through the rituals, the communion; with my mind on how soon I could get away to the blonde I was planning to bed down. But after you came I could only think of how you had looked at Allie's the night before in that pale blue satin gown held up by two thin straps on your slender body, your red hair barely containing its curls in the sparkling combs. So I would skip the blonde and go to Ben's to try to get a glimpse of you.

When Ben sent me to you during your last month of pregnancy everything changed and nothing changed; I wanted desperately to leave Ben, but couldn't because I couldn't leave you. I lived for those chaste hours we spent together during those weeks, helplessly stuck in a no-man's land of love.

Now that we will spend the rest of our lives together in truth, love and freedom, I guess we can thank Ben for our newfound happiness. But let's not. Let's thank God.

Chapter 18

When I hurried to our street corner on the Monday before we were scheduled to leave, Bobby wasn't there. I told myself that waiting, he drove around the block. I told myself that he was detained with a last-minute telephone call. Just calm down and wait, I told myself. But people don't stand around on street corners in our neighborhood, and after fifteen or twenty minutes I began to feel conspicuous under the street lamp. I walked around the block three or four times watching for the Pierce Arrow. I passed a man walking his dog and said good evening.

A cold wind had come up in that sudden way spring in Cleveland can turn back into winter, and at ten o'clock, chilled to the bone, I went home. I called Bobby from the kitchen telephone. No answer. I felt a clutch of fear. Stop this, I told myself. Ben doesn't know about us. There's a perfectly reasonable explanation—trouble with the car or his mother got sick or Ben sent him somewhere, maybe even out of town. And of course he couldn't call me. I went upstairs to bed. And lay there, wide-awake with mounting terror, thinking the unthinkable.

Sleeping that night I heard Ben laugh an old woman's cackle while I searched for Bobby, afraid to open the red door that stood at the end of a dark corridor. Startled awake, I waited for my pulse to quiet down. But I couldn't fall back asleep and after a while heard a car pull into the driveway. I got up and looked out the window expecting to see Ben coming home. But the Packard was already parked there, another car had pulled up behind it, and as I watched, the headlights blinked off and I could make out the shape of a man as he walked into the basement entrance. I got out of bed and crept noiselessly into the hall and down the stairs to the basement in my pink nightgown, first one bare foot then the other, silent as a cat. A faucet was dripping somewhere. The basement smelled of starch and ironed shirts. I heard voices from the reception room, ducked under the sheets strung on a clothesline, and slipped into the pantry.

"Gold," the stranger was shouting, "you owe me a grand! I want it and I want it now!"

"Quiet down!" Ben hissed. "You'll wake everyone!"

The man lowered his voice and straining to hear, I could only catch: "pay up time." Then: "contract" or maybe "contact" and what sounded like "proof...newspaper." Then Ben said, "Tipped" or "ripped him off." Pressing my ear to the wall, I heard the stranger say, "Pierce Arrow...bottom...river," and the words blew me against the shelves of stacked peaches and canned tomatoes, hurting my back.

I flew out of the pantry screaming like a madwoman. Ben was closing the door behind the man and wheeled around to me. I sprang at him with whirling arms. He grabbed my wrists and pinned them to my sides. I kept on screaming. I screamed and screamed silently with my mouth open.

"Ah, Kate," Ben said, shaking his head. "Why'd you do this? Why'd you go and listen? You didn't have to know. You didn't have to. I was going to tell you I sent Bobby out of town on a job. Why'd you go and spoil everything," he moaned, his voice trailing off sorrowfully.

There was a wildfire of rage and grief whipping around in my chest like some rampaging, untamed beast, beating up into my head, burning my heart; I thought I would burst. I thought my anguish would explode my body shattering Ben and me. I wanted it to. I wanted to die, taking Ben and this place of death with me. Wailing, my head wobbling, my bones unable to sustain the weight of my grief, my knees turned to rubber, my back to mush. I melted into the floor. Ben reached for me. I lifted my foot aiming for his groin. Dodging nimbly, he got my hand and pulled me up, but I was a moaning rag doll and slid out of his grip like spilling blood, a tangle of limbs and hair, my face and neck and nightgown sodden with tears, my wails soaring higher and higher gone somewhere off on a life of their own.

Then Ben was on his knees holding a glass of whisky to my mouth. I raised my head and tossed it down in a gulp. I saw the table and whitewashed walls and chair and they seemed to have a pitiless message for me about Ben and Bobby and myself, about mendacity and treachery and the power of Ben's seduction and my own lethal choices. I lay my head back down on the floor, and in a strange kind of alchemy my whisky-numbed brain slowly became as uncluttered and clear as ice, and I had a revelation of pure evil hiding under a splendid smile and a pocketful of money and lies and declarations of love. At least it was the truth. In the midst of my chilling vision I felt an insane stab of relief for the truth.

Ben tried to help me up off the floor, but I waved him off and slithered on my stomach to the couch. Pulling myself up, I sat carefully and held my glass up for a refill.

"Believe me, Kate," Ben said, pouring. "I didn't want to do it. I had to. He gave me no choice. You think I'm going to let him fuck my wife and live? What kind of a dimwit do you take me for?"

I sat, sipping the whisky, breathing its heat, becoming nicely numb.

"I trusted him like a brother," he went on, filling my glass again. "So he double-crosses me with my wife. *My wife!* That's the thanks I get. But he underestimated me. So did you. Because I found out." He turned to me with neon-yellow eyes. "Did you think I wouldn't know about the two of you? You don't know me yet? All I had to do was wait for the right time for the hit—like when he went to church with his mother."

"So when are you going to kill me?"

He looked puzzled. "Why would I kill you? You're my wife; you belong to me—I don't kill what I own. We'll have babies, we'll go to Allie's, to New York like before, everything the same." He began to pace. "Although I have to tell you, not quite. No, ma'am, not quite. I got to watch you don't cheat on me again. So I hired this guy, highly recommended—in fact he's a second or third cousin to the Sarsenis, forty-four years old, nice guy, tough as nails. Name's Joey or Jimmy, something like that. He'll be your driver and watchdog, take you shopping, to the beauty shop, to see your mother, anywhere you want." He stopped pacing and looked at me. "I promise you, you will not be out of his sight for a minute, day or night."

I stared at him. His shirt was whiter than new snow, the diamonds in his tie and cuffs dazzled my eyes, his face grew longer as I watched. I saw each blunt black hair on his face. I saw the red veins in the whites of his eyes. I saw his pores as big as craters. It was a face in a fun house mirror.

I am drunk, I thought, peering into my empty glass. I felt pretty good. I was no longer responsible for anything. Nothing was my fault.

Suddenly everything in my stomach was on its way up. I dashed into the bathroom and vomited into the toilet. Then I threw up again. And again. I couldn't stop. Everything I couldn't digest for the past months lay purged and when nothing was left to vomit I kept on gagging helplessly until I finally sank to the bathroom floor, covered with sweat, smelling vomit, the tile floor cool on my cheek, drunk, floating, lighter than air, emptied.

Ben came in and helped me to my feet. I pushed him aside and staggered out of the bathroom. He took my arm, but I shook it off and continued my wobbly walk to the sofa. He stood there, looking at me.

"Get away from me," I said, just before I passed out

* * *

I woke, still on the sofa. Someone had covered me with a blanket. Trying not to jar my aching head, I stood up slowly in my vomit-stained pink nightgown and peered at the clock in Ben's office. Six-thirty. I was afraid to look at Bobby's dark desk. I heard the same chirping of robins and wrens that warbled when Bobby was alive.

Upstairs, Francine was in her attic room, Ben nowhere to be seen. The quiet house hummed in my ears. I gulped two aspirins, scrubbed my teeth, showered, and dressed, wondering why Ben went out so early. I tried to remember what the stranger had said last night. Something about proof; read your morning newspaper, the man said. On my way downstairs, I stopped. Yes. Of course. Unable to wait, impatient for the proof, looking for the body in black and white, Ben went out for the newspaper an hour earlier than usual. But why did he want proof? Is Ben afraid Bobby paid off the hit man? He knows he's not dealing with the Sarseni brothers here. Bobby's so quick, so savvy—Ben knows he could have bribed him—that's why he wouldn't pay the assassin last night—that's why he rushed out for proof at dawn. He thinks Bobby could be alive. I felt like laughing wildly. Then I was on my knees, saying my mother's Hebrew prayers, willing Bobby alive, praying Bobby alive, begging for Bobby's life while entreaties to my mother's God I thought long forgotten came tumbling from my terrified lips again and again as if their sheer number could make up for my lapsed years, my fallen years, and provide mercy and forgiveness and Bobby's young, sweet life.

Face soaked, I struggled to my feet like an old woman and stood at the window, watching. I hoped Ben would never come. I did not want him to come. I did not want the news. I stood there waiting and watching until I saw Ben walk into the driveway holding a folded newspaper.

I turned away from the window and went down the stairs to the basement with shaking knees.

Ben looked startled when he saw me. "Now, Kate—"

I grabbed the paper out of his hand and read the headline:

SENATE PASSES VETERANS COMPENSATION ACT OVER PRESIDENT HOOVER'S VETO

He's alive. He's alive. My legs almost gave way. Then my eye caught a smaller article in the bottom right hand corner:

BODY FOUND IN AUTOMOBILE AT BOTTOM OF CUYAHOGA RIVER

Cleveland—Acting on an anonymous tip received early this morning, police discovered a

Pierce Arrow automobile sunk in the Cuyahoga River offshore at Second Ave. The body of a male in his twenties or thirties was behind the wheel, a bullet hole in the back of the head. The medical examiner estimated the killing took place approximately 48 hours ago. There was no identification in the car or on the body...

I let the paper drop to the floor.

Ben picked it up and sat on the couch. The blanket was still there from the night before. I could smell the vomit. "Believe me, Kate," he said, earnestly, "I know how you feel. Listen, don't you think I'm upset? I'm upset plenty. The man I trusted like a brother double-crossed me with my wife. *MY WIFE!*" He looked up at me where I was still standing. "I know you don't believe me, Kate; you're too upset now to believe me, but I want you to know this was his own fault, not mine."

He got up and reached for me. I backed away. "Kate," he said, dropping his hands to his sides. "I told you. We're going on like before, husband and wife. We'll have children. The only difference is now you got a driver and watchdog." He narrowed his amber eyes. "Considering the alternatives at my disposal, you haven't come out too bad."

"Alternatives at your disposal. That you didn't kill me, too."

"Well, you broke our marriage vows, didn't you? You cheated on me, didn't you? So yeah, I did have alternatives at my disposal—as you well know—that may I remind you, I didn't choose. And therefore expect some appreciation and cooperation from you."

I stared at him. He looked like a regular person. I looked at his hands. No blood.

"Come. Kate. Sit down."

But I didn't seem able to move.

"You don't look so good," he said. "You're white as a sheet." He narrowed his eyes. "You, my dear, have a hangover."

He disappeared into the bathroom and returned with two aspirins and a glass of water. "Here. And for God's sake, sit down."

I sat down obediently in the leather armchair and reached for the aspirins and glass. I actually smiled at him.

"Breakfast's ready," Francine called down the stairs.

"Try to get something down, Kate. Food'll help—at least a cup of coffee."

I sat stiffly in the chair gripping the water glass.

Red-faced, his hands became fists. "I'm making allowances for you. You aren't yourself," he said, in a breaking voice. "I know that. But I'm warning you," he said, breathing hard, "don't push me." He reached for the newspaper. Then he turned on his heel and left the room.

Feeling nothing but an odd emptiness, as if I were hollow, I went upstairs and lay down on the guest room bed. After a while I started thinking about the newspaper article. It said Bobby had been dead forty-eight hours. That would put the murder, let's see, on Sunday. Bobby always went to twelve o'clock Mass with his mother on Sundays, then back to her apartment for lunch. He never missed a Sunday. Ben knew it, I knew it, we all knew it. I imagined Bobby coming out of his mother's apartment after lunch, a perfect target for the man waiting in his car. Let's see, that would be about two o'clock. The man gets out of his car, approaches Bobby, and puts his arm around him as if they're buddies. He sticks a gun against his side under his coat. (early season in Cleveland is cool, you know, and Bobby would be wearing a coat.) The man then makes Bobby sit in the Pierce Arrow and gets behind the wheel. No, wait a minute. He wouldn't do that. He needs to keep his gun on Bobby. So he makes Bobby drive, jamming the gun at his side, low, because it is broad daylight. The man directs him. But where? Surely not to his own place, probably to some room he rented for the occasion, no doubt near the river so that he wouldn't have to drive far, later. If you're going to murder someone you have to think of getting rid of the body, don't you? When they arrive at a dilapidated building the man prods Bobby with his gun up the dark steps. Inside a room, he locks the door and pulls the torn shade down on the dirty window. Perhaps Bobby now regrets not taking his chance and jumping out of the car in daylight, in traffic, at a stoplight. It is now, say, two-thirty or three o'clock. The man has to keep him in this room until dark. So how do they pass the time? Playing cards on the rickety bed? Talking about baseball? Politics? Just sort of getting acquainted? Bobby tries to make a deal; he offers money. The man refuses. Obviously. Is that what they call honor among thieves? When it gets dark (about seven o'clock these days—what was I doing Sunday night at seven? Eating dinner with Ben? Reading the newspaper? For the life of me I couldn't remember.) The man takes Bobby downstairs in the darkness, puts him behind the wheel of the Pierce Arrow, and gets in the back seat. He presses the gun to Bobby's head and directs him down Second Street to the Cuyahoga River. (I wondered, ashamed, if Bobby was thinking of me.) When they arrive at the river (it is a short ride), he shoots him in the back of the head. He no doubt has a silencer on his gun. (I knew about silencers from the gun Bobby gave me.) Bobby slumps over the steering wheel. There is blood running down and pooling on the floor. Does it ooze from his ears and nose? Does it get on the soft white leather seat? Do his brains? Is there really such a thing as a death rattle? I gagged, but there was nothing in my stomach to vomit.

The man gets out of the car and puts the stick shift in neutral. He looks around and then pushes, pushes, pushes, until the car slides into the river. It is heavy, of course, and the man is breathing hard as he watches it disappear. The automobile sinks rapidly into the black river. The man brushes off his trousers and straightens his tie; a job well done. Then he walks up to Euclid Avenue and hails a cab.

I imagined Bobby dead. I saw him floating inside the Pierce Arrow with a nice little smile on his face as if he is saying, *Look, Red, don't worry, this isn't so bad, being dead is okay.* Then I pictured him behind the wheel with a scream shaping his mouth that he didn't have time to make. His mouth is a black hole, his eyes transparent blue glass, his hands white as frozen snow. Did he die fast or slow? Did his hands claw at the air?

* * *

I don't know how long I lay there that morning, but after a while I realized I was waiting for Ben and Sam to leave. When I heard the Packard back out of the driveway, I went to my black hat where I had hidden the gun Bobby gave me in its deep crown, under my journal. There was a plan forming in my brewing brain that involved Bobby's dead brother's clothes hidden in a hatbox in the back of my closet that I had been going to wear during our escape on the *Franconia*. In my scheming mind, the clothes and the gun were plotting retribution.

* * *

The next night, after Ben and Sam left, I went outside with a flashlight to the alley that Ben used for a shortcut on his morning walks to Jake's newsstand for the morning newspaper. Looking for a place to hide, I found a recessed doorway to a closed shoe repair shop.

* * *

"Mrs. Gold?" Francine called the next morning, knocking on the door. "Breakfast."

"Come on in, Francine—just leave the tray on the dresser."

"Yes, ma'am."

"Thank you."

I had watched Ben dress that morning in one of his silk suits, taking longer than usual to select a tie. Finally he settled on a design of red flowers on a blue background from the dozens that hung in his closet. Knotting it carefully in the mirror, he arranged his black fedora on his head, angling it perfectly.

"I'm going for the paper," he said, leaving the room.

I dashed out of bed and into Danny Keane's clothes, piling my hair under his cap. The gun fit nicely in my pocket. I pulled on my gloves, the only pair I had besides my winter mittens, vaguely noting the irony of their white kid elegance.

The newsstand where Ben bought the *Cleveland Plain Dealer* every morning was at the corner of Westchester and Kenmore. He was a man of such regular habits that I knew exactly when he would be returning, the newspaper tucked under his arm, looking forward to his breakfast of scrambled eggs with his newspaper propped up on the coffee pot. On a rare occasion, if a headline interested him, he would stop walking and read the article, which if he did now would dangerously throw off my timing.

I flattened myself against the shoemaker's doorway that I had discovered the night before, took the gun out of my pocket, pushed off the safety, and waited. Right on time, in exactly eight minutes, I heard Ben's footsteps. As he approached, I stepped out and pointed the gun at his face. Before pulling the trigger, I pulled off my cap and let my hair fall loose.

His mouth opened in shocked recognition. "Kate!"

I shot. He bled on the red flowers of his silk tie. I dropped the gun and ran, tucking my hair back under the cap.

Back home, I slipped up the back steps into our bedroom, laid my gloves in the drawer next to my fur-lined mittens, and changed back into my nightgown. I put Danny's clothes back into the hatbox, (later dropping them off at the Salvation Army). Francine, I knew, would be knocking on the door any minute for the breakfast tray. But it was still standing on the dresser where she had left it, the food untouched. I wasted precious time staring at the now-cold poached eggs, coffee and toast, understanding that even a bite of toast or a forkful of eggs would make me vomit. Violently. For the first time that morning I panicked. Should I tell Francine that I'm not hungry this morning, or maybe that I'm not feeling well? But I always ate everything on the breakfast tray, morning after morning, and everything, *everything*, must appear to be absolutely normal when the police question Francine. Staring at the tray full of food, my mind stopped by panic, helplessly feeling precious time slip away as the clock on the dresser ticked loudly as a drum beat, I didn't know what to do. Then I felt my stomach rise, empty as it was. Inspired, I flushed the eggs and coffee down the toilet. The toast presented a problem—I had to tear it into little pieces to get it to flush, which took too long because my hands were shaking.

Still in my nightgown, I rushed into bed with the tray, its dishes now innocently emptied, waiting to become a bereaved widow, my beloved husband probably shot down by Francis Sarseni in retaliation for the murder of his brothers, who was also wanted by the police for the robbery and murder of a grocery store clerk.

It seemed like seconds later—but in my state could have been longer—that Francine came into the bedroom after a polite knock on the door and picked up the tray from my lap. I pulled back the covers so she would see me in my nightgown, said thank you, Francine, that was delicious, as I stretched and pretended to yawn.

Francine left with the tray and I lay back on the pillows with a feeling of such nervous relief, it was as if I had finally crawled to the top of Mount Everest on my hands and knees. There still remained the heart-stopping trip down the mountain. I knew there was still more to come, but meanwhile my feeling of the moment's deliverance was so exquisite I breathed it in and let myself sink deeply into the pillows, waiting again for the knock on the door.

It came soon enough.

"Mrs. Gold, there are two police officers here to see you," Francine said, coming into the bedroom.

"Police officers? Whatever for?"

"They didn't say. Just they needed to see you."

"I must have dozed off—tell them I'll be down as soon as I get my robe on."

"Yes, ma'am."

It was still early, not yet nine. Two police officers were downstairs waiting for me, and I reasoned that under those circumstances one would wear a robe.

They were standing awkwardly just inside the door when I arrived in the living room. It was a cloudy morning and a light rain had left the room dim, but I recognized them as the cops on Ben's payroll who came that night when we were hiding out. One was tall and dark-skinned, the other blond and freckled, who looked too young to already be corrupted by Ben.

"What can I do for you?" I asked. I remembered Ben asking one of them about his baby. "How's your youngster doing?"

"Ma'am," the tall one said. "Mrs. Gold. Please sit down."

"Why? Is something wrong? I think we already sent our donation to the Police Retirement Fund."

"Please, ma'am," he said again. "I think you'd better sit." He cleared his throat.

I obediently sat down on the couch.

Sam came lumbering into the room and stopped short when he saw the policemen. "What are you two doing here?"

"We're here to talk to Mrs. Gold."

"Francine!" he shouted. "Has Ben showed up for breakfast?"

She came into the living room drying her hands on a towel. "No, his breakfast's waiting on him."

Sam turned to me sitting on the couch. "Where is he? It's after nine—is he sick or something?"

"He went to get the newspaper."

"Yeah, but he's always in the office by now."

"Who are you?" The young policeman asked Sam.

"Sam Ginsburg."

"What are you doing here?"

'What I'm doing here? I'm doing what I always do here. I work for Ben Gold. Ben Gold's my boss."

"Then you'd better sit down, too." He turned to Francine. "You, also."

"What the hell's going on?" Sam demanded, as Francine sat down on the wing chair by the window.

The tall one cleared his throat. "I'm afraid I have some very bad news. Ben Gold's body was found shot dead in the alley behind Westchester Street." He looked at his watch. "Forty minutes ago."

I had been practicing in my mind how to play the role of a bereaved widow, afraid I wasn't a good enough actress, that I wouldn't be able to bring it off. But I needn't have worried. All I had to do was think of Bobby.

"No!" I screamed. "No!" And I started to sob. I thought about Bobby and sobbed. My grief knocked my head down on the couch. I lay there, caught in a vise of anguish over my loss of Bobby, of love, of life. I could not stop sobbing. Finally, as the two policemen, Francine, and Sam watched, my sobs turned into a kind of whimper. I lay there making the moaning sounds of a wounded animal.

Francine mopped up my face with one of Ben's linen monogrammed handkerchiefs and covered me with a blanket. I dimly heard one of the policemen ask Francine for the name and telephone number of my doctor, and in a few minutes his voice on the telephone to Doctor Donavan, explaining the situation of Ben's murder, my overwhelming grief and need for a sedative. Remembering that the doctor had to be helped, limping, out of my hospital room after Ben knocked him down, I almost had to stuff the handkerchief in my mouth so I wouldn't start smiling over the doctor's probable lack of sympathy at Ben's untimely death. I thought if the combination of my suppressed smile and uncontrollable sobbing meant I was finally going crazy, it was okay, because Ben's departure from this world by my own hand was worth it.

"The drug store will deliver a prescription for you," the young cop told me.

"I know who done this!" Sam shouted, sliding his narrow black eyes to the tall policemen. "Frank Sarseni! I'll get that son of a bitch!" he said, dashing to the door where he was stopped by the young cop's arm, exposing his holstered gun. "Homicide needs to question you down at the station."

That made me want to smile again. They'd get as much information out of Sam as they would a rock, or Ben's corpse. The tall one turned to Francine. "We need to question you, too." He looked at me, lying on the couch under the blanket. "Take your medicine, Mrs. Gold, and rest. The detectives will be back to talk to you later."

The four of them left and I watched them through the window as they got into the cruiser and it pulled away.

Chapter 19

After the probate procedure, I was handed the key to Ben's safety deposit box in the vault of the Cleveland Trust Bank. The clerk discretely left as I took the box into the curtained alcove reserved for such privacy. I opened it and found piles of bills neatly stacked and bound with rubber bands. It took me a long time to count them, because not believing my eyes, I had to go through the one million two hundred and twenty dollars twice, and then once again. The thousand dollar bills were crisp and new; the ten's and twenties wrinkled and folded, looking as innocent as any you would get in change at the grocery or drug store—no blood. I stuffed as many bills in my handbag as it would hold, casting aside my own corruption over the eagerness, the thrill, in getting my hands on what was, I knew, blood money. I slid the box back in its place on the wall among the others. (It was, after all, 1932, and I wasn't about to deposit the money in a bank—not with all the failures and closings around the country.) Then, with a banging heart and sweating palms, I rang for the clerk to lock the box, hand me my key, and let me out.

I had been in the bank so long, that when I stepped outside, fog had moved in like a gauzy veil shrouding the familiar neighborhood and adding to my feeling of being lost in a dream. A cab turned up and still in a trance, I climbed in.

At home with the key to Safety Deposit Box #829 safely tucked into my handbag, all I could do was pace, my youth burning in me, dizzy with choices. I could finally go to college! I could write stories! I could take care of my mother! I could take care of Francine! And Francine's whole family! I could sell this house and buy another one! I could travel! I could finally get rid of Sam, who had been hanging around during the probate process with nothing to do. Finally, I sat down, too stunned to do anything else, until dusk fell and I heard Sam's heavy step approaching.

I turned on the lamp at my elbow. "Hi, Sam. You're just the man I want to see. I'm putting the house on the market so you can go ahead and clean out the offices." Let him examine the sick secrets, the murderous strategies, the buried and the shrouded. There was nothing I wanted to see. I had freed myself of violence. Violently.

"What's your hurry?" he said.

My hurry. As if I hadn't been counting the days, hours, minutes, walking the rooms of this strange, hollow house with Bobby gone, Ben gone, Maggie gone; as if the time would never come that I could escape this house of death.

"I wanted to wait until Ben's case was officially closed," I told him.

"Ben's case ain't officially closed until I get that son of a bitch Frank Sarseni! I gotta get him before the cops do."

"You'd better be careful," I said, thinking that now, sooner or later, Sam would be gone, too.

"Don't you worry, I'll get him," he said. "A piece of cake."

"A piece of cake? Why?"

"Because he's a kid, the youngest Sarseni brother. Can't be more than seventeen or eighteen and a murderer already."

"Well, Sam, good luck. I'm sure you'll get another job—you know everyone in the business."

"Hey, wait a minute! You need me."

"Whatever for?"

He thought for a few moments. "Well, to drive you places."

"No, Sam, I already let Jimmy go."

"Jimmy? The guy Ben hired to drive you?"

"I don't need a driver—I'm going to learn." I held out my hand. "I'll give you a thousand dollars tomorrow for your severance pay."

He took my hand. I thought I saw his narrow black eyes moisten. "I can't believe this. We was like family here—you, Ben, and me. Even Bobby." He released my hand and turned away, shaking his head. "I'll clean out the desks tomorrow," he muttered, lumbering to the door.

And he was gone, the house silent again. Well, Francine was still here. And my mother. Vivian at Pembroke. She was a junior now. A college girl. Sitting in classes, studying for a blue book exam, going out on dates. I never had a date. Just a husband. I was an adulterer. A murderer. A mother (for almost three hours). What would Mrs. Joseph say to all that?

Thinking of Vivian, I saw that our close friendship had existed in another life and felt a stab of sadness at its loss. Realizing how much I missed her, I closed my eyes, trying to forgive myself for that day two years ago when we quarreled about Ben, and to forgive Vivian for being right about him. Now ashamed of all the lies I had written her, I picked up the phone to call Mrs. Joseph for her phone number. But suddenly feeling the abyss that had grown between Vivian's schoolgirl innocence and my deadly mistakes, I put the phone down. I didn't know how to cross the gulf.

Chapter 20

My father took me to a wake once when I was a kid—I never knew who the dead person was, except that I saw my daddy actually cry when he got the news over the telephone. I had never seen a grown-up man cry before and it scared me—but not nearly as much as seeing the dead man lying in an open coffin in his own living room. The house was jammed with people—everyone drinking and laughing and admiring the corpse and saying things like, Don't he look peaceful and God bless his soul—stuff like that. My father raised his glass and said, Here's to you, Joey. There was so much celebration I was afraid the corpse would get up from his white satin pillow and join the party.

But when a Jew dies, if the friends paying a condolence call to the family have a drink or two, someone is sure to admonish them sternly: *This isn't a PARTY!* as the widow sits long-faced. If she is crying, so much the better. Also unlike Catholics, Jews always bury their dead quickly.

Ben died on Friday so the funeral had to be on Sunday. That left little time to find his mother in New York, and any other of Ben's family she knew of. I had to get a black dress and shoes appropriate for a grieving widow. I had to make the necessary arrangements with the funeral home. I had to order flowers to cover Ben's casket.

But first, his mother. I remembered her last name—Bernstein—but couldn't think of her first. Something with an S—Sonia? Sandra? There must have been hundreds of Bernsteins in the New York telephone book—I had to remember it. And then I did! Sarah. Sarah Bernstein. Sam had told me it was Sarah. I went to the library, got the Manhattan telephone book, and saw, to my dismay, almost one entire column of Sarah Bernsteins. Then I remembered that Ben said she constantly checked the Plaza Hotel to see when he would be in New York. Wouldn't she leave her phone number with the hotel to be called when he had reservations? It was worth a try, and when I called the Plaza explaining the nature of my sudden need to reach Mrs. Bernstein, they provided it immediately.

* * *

"Hello, Mrs. Bernstein?'

"Who's this?"

"It's Kate Gold."

"Gold? You're related to Benny?"

"His wife. Remember? You and I met in the Plaza when you came to see Ben that time?"

Silence. Deep breathing. Finally, "Yeah. I remember."

"Mrs. Bernstein, I'm afraid I have very bad news," I said.

"So what bad news. If you ask me everything is bad news. All I hear is bad news. Mr. Lankowski had a heart attack. A nice man, lived in the apartment next door, had a heart attack. I heard the sirens."

"No, no, you don't understand—"

"I understand. So tell me your bad news."

"Mrs. Bernstein," I said, "Ben died."

"What? What did you say?"

I cleared my throat. "I said Ben died."

"Died? How did he die?"

"He was shot."

"You killed him!" she shouted.

I was afraid I would fall off my chair. I fell off my chair.

"Hello? Hello?" she shouted.

I got up, still clutching the telephone. "I dropped the phone," I told her. My hands were sweating and shaking so much I could hardly hold the receiver in my ear. "How could you say such a thing?"

"Because I know you shiksas. You want this, you want that, you want a mansion, you want everything you see and he takes chances, he gets mixed up with the bad people to buy you things. I saw you with the jewels, the furs. Fox! White! Down to your ankles! Diamonds in your hair! A chiffon dress with beads, yet! Don't worry, I saw."

"Mrs. Bernstein, who was the family in Cleveland that took you, your husband, and Ben in years ago?"

"I can't remember."

"It was when you moved from Detroit to Cleveland."

"Oh them. My husband's brother."

"What's his name?"

"What you want it for?"

I wanted to wring her neck. "To invite him to his nephew's funeral!"

"He won't come."

"His name, please!"

"You don't have to holler!"

"Please."

"Jacob Shulzman."

"Mrs. Bernstein, the funeral is Thursday. I checked the schedule and if you take the night train you'll arrive in Cleveland tomorrow morning at seven AM. Sam will pick you up and bring you to the house."

"Sam? Who's Sam?"

"Sam Ginsburg, Ben's friend."

"Is it a Jewish funeral?"

"Yes, Rabbi Pincus."

"A shiksa gets a rabbi?"

"Mrs. Bernstein, I am not a shiksa. My mother is Jewish."

"What about your father?"

"Catholic."

"So you're a shiksa."

"Goodbye, Mrs. Bernstein."

One more call to make. I looked into the Cleveland telephone book, and there was his name: Jacob Shulzman on Chapman Road with his telephone number.

"Mr. Shulzman?"

"Yes, this is Mr. Shulzman."

"This is Kate Gold."

"Benny's wife?"

"Was. I'm calling to tell you—"

"You don't have to tell me. It was all over the papers. The man who shot him should get a medal. I'd like to shake his hand and give him a medal."

"The funeral is—"

"He was nothing but *tsuris* from the day he was born. We took them in, my brother, his wife and son, room and board. We have a small house. I am not a rich man, but it was family, and you do for family. So the son starts running with gangs. Do you know what my brother did with the *gelt* that *gonef* gave him? He threw it down the toilet before I could get my hands on it. He broke my brother's heart. He killed my brother, a good man, a pious man. My Rosalie, a *baleboste*, she should rest in peace, cooked, cleaned, washed and ironed and his *meshuge* wife never lifted a finger."

"Mr. Shulzman, I just want to tell you the funeral is tomorrow at two o'clock at the Berkowitz Funeral Home. Do you need directions?"

"Do I need directions? I don't need directions. I don't give a goddamn where it is because I wouldn't go if it was across the street. I wouldn't go if it was next door. If you don't mind my asking, how could you marry such a man?"

"That's a very good question. Good bye, Mr. Shulzman."

* * *

The telephone was in the kitchen, perched on a small table. It also had a chair from which I made telephone calls. As I hung up, Francine walked in and began to cut up a chicken for soup.

I looked at her in her white uniform and realized that I had never seen her in anything else, except for the same blue dress she always wore on her days off.

I picked up the phone and called Sam. "I need you to drive us to Milgrims. How soon can you get here?"

"Us? Who's this us?"

"Francine and me."

Francine turned around from the stove and stared at me.

"Francine?" Sam said. "To that fancy shop?"

"How soon can you get here?" I asked again.

"Twenty minutes."

"And tomorrow, pick up Ben's mother at seven AM at the Terminal Train Station. You remember her, right?"

"How could I forget such a *mushuge*? I'll be there."

After I hung up, Francine said, "I ain't goin' to no Milgrims."

"Francine, we both need a dress to wear to the funeral. It'll be okay—you'll be with me."

She folded her arms. "No way. No, ma'am. Girl, I ain't goin to no white peoples' shop."

To my surprise, I started to cry. It was all too much, too much. I put my face down in my hands and wept.

I felt Francine's hand on my shoulder. "Don't cry. Please don't cry. You just been through too much." She handed me the clean handkerchief she always wore in the pocket of her uniform.

I blew my nose and looked up. "Francine, I would never let anything bad happen to you. Please. Go change out of your uniform."

She looked at me. "I can't. I'm too nervous."

"Please. I'll come up and help you."

"No, you already done enough helpin'," she muttered as she left the room. "I'm gonna hate this."

"Hurry up," I said.

* * *

As Francine and I entered Milgrims, a saleslady approached us. She was in her forties, fashionably dressed in a navy blue dress with a white collar and high-heeled pumps. I thought her black hair looked dyed.

"We would like to see what you have in dresses," I said. "Miss Francine Boyd wears a size twelve, and I'm a ten."

"But she's colored," the saleslady said, glancing at Francine. "We don't wait on coloreds."

Francine turned around to leave, but I grabbed her arm and pulled her back. "If you don't wait on her, I'll have you fired."

"*You* get me *fired*? Don't make me laugh."

"I will get you fired. I'm Ben Gold's widow and I have friends."

She turned pale under her makeup. "I have to see the manager," she said, rushing away.

In minutes a man arrived, followed by the saleslady. "Welcome, Mrs. Gold," he said. "Please accept my condolences over your great loss. And may I say any friends of your late husband's are friends of mine and we're happy to serve you." He snapped his fingers. "Selma, take care of these ladies."

"Yes, Mr. Hoover."

Francine selected a paisley print in shades of blue and green, and I choose a demure high-necked black silk, appropriate for the funeral of my beloved husband. In the shoe department, Francine surprised me by picking out a pair of high-heeled red satin shoes that, judging by the expression on her face of pure joy, thrilled her. My choice had to be a pair of low-heeled black.

We left the shop with our packages and met Sam, waiting at the curb in the Packard.

* * *

Dressing for the funeral, I topped off my outfit with the wide-brimmed black straw hat where I had hidden, in its deep crown, my journal and the gun Bobby gave me. At first I couldn't think of a safe enough place to hide it. (Under the mattress? No, Francine changed the bed sheets. Buried in my lingerie? No, too obvious.) Finally, I found the perfect place—in plain sight in the crown of the hat that sat innocently on the shelf of my clothes closet.

Now, I put it on my head, pulling the brim over my eyes in case tears failed me during the appropriate moments. Then I went to the telephone, called the Fresh Cut Floral Shop on Beakely Road, and ordered Ben's casket to be covered with roses and gardenias.

Francine, in her new dress, Sam in his rumpled suit, and I, in my widow's weeds, climbed into the limo waiting at the curb, sent by the funeral home. We picked up my mother, who seemed sober. She was wearing the same brown dress printed with lilac flowers she had warn to Vivien's graduation party. I wished I had thought to buy her a new dress, too, but after a respectful mourning period decided to take her shopping. We'd go to Halle's Department Store and buy her an entirely new wardrobe—dresses, underwear, nightgowns, a robe, a nice winter coat, a pair of shoes that fit her feet—and throw out those unlaced oxfords she clattered around in for most of my life.

The funeral home, in its pristine, shining perfection, had so many enormous vases of fake roses, lilacs, tulips, and mums, it was as if, even faux, the undertakers tried to convince the bereaved, and perhaps even God, as being a worthy place from which the Taken would be sent on their final journey.

The anteroom was already crowded with Ben's colleagues, friends, and enemies, as is the custom. Mobsters traditionally pay their respects to each other at such times, perhaps today feeling immune to Ben's sad fate due to their superior use of the tools of the trade. Or, in their arrogance, believed that although Ben was known to be smart, they were smarter. After all, weren't they here, paying their respects in their black silk suits and polished dress shoes, while Ben lay in his coffin?

I didn't know most of the people, although I did recognize some of the men who had visited Ben's basement office. Today, in respect to the deceased, they devoutly held their fedoras in both hands, as, with little bows, they offered me their sympathy. Which I acknowledged with a grief-stricken nod.

Their women came, too; some I had met at Allie's, others I had never seen before, like the middle-aged Italian ladies with dark hair and eyes and swelling breasts. I wondered if they knew the truth about their husbands' work. I wondered what they told their children. The flashy blondes with made-up faces and glittering jewelry, their dazzle shining through their subdued clothes, were moving restlessly among the mourners, turning heads.

One of them approached me, "So sorry for your loss," she said, sticking out her hand. "Mary Nickolatta."

"Thank you for coming," I said, taking her hand. She was wearing a short black satin that someone must have sewn her into, and ropes of pearls that hung down to her ample cleavage. Spike heels showed off her beautiful legs. She looked me up and down, took my arm, and pulled me aside. "Honey," she said in a low voice, "I need to take you shopping. You're too young and pretty to wear an old lady's dress like that. I don't care if it is a funeral, you got to dress up better. We'll have lunch at the Theatrical Grill and shop our heads off. Okay?"

"Maybe later," I said politely.

"Yeah, I guess it would be unseemly to go too soon." She pulled my hat off. "Look at you! A natural redhead with blue eyes! No wonder you got Ben Gold. I gotta hand it to you—he was a sexy rich guy."

Furious, I grabbed my hat from her hand and put it back on my head. Looking at her heavy makeup and hard eyes, I saw what I could have become at her age. Didn't I glory in my slinky low-cut dresses, jewels, high heels, furs? Wasn't I right at home in the house that looked like an expensive bordello? And didn't I walk with pride on Ben's arm into speakeasies with diamond combs sparkling in my hair? Who was I to judge?

"I'll call you," Mary Nickolatta said as she turned away, walking carefully in her three-inch heels.

If Maggie had lived I would have had to leave Ben, and he would have killed me before he'd let me take his baby away. But I would never let Ben raise Maggie. So I would have had to kill him before he killed me, and I'd be standing here even if I'd never laid eyes on Bobby Keane. I must have been born to kill Ben Gold. I must have been brought into the world to rid it of his evil. It must have been my destiny. Because here I was, having achieved what Ben's enemies and several professional killers had tried and failed to do.

The funeral director appeared at my side and asked if I wished to go into the private room set aside for the family of the deceased. Since Ben's mother hadn't shown up at the train station, and his uncle refused to attend, his family consisted only of me. I had no wish to be by myself in such a room, and declined, sitting in the first row of the pitifully empty chairs.

The mourners had filed into the large sanctuary with the podium for the Rabbi, and the Sacred Torah ahead. Someone somewhere was playing an organ, an instrument I have always disliked. Every seat was filled and those without chairs stood at the rear of the room. The room murmured, the organ droned on, we waited for the rabbi.

Rabbi Pincus finally made his entrance in a black robe and yarmulke, looking very important, busy, and somewhat annoyed at his vocation of dealing with death and God. Or maybe it was Ben Gold himself in the flower-covered casket in front of him, and the well-known deadly facts of his life and death that put the rabbi in a bad mood. Or his irritation could have come from the notorious identities of the mourners—a Who's Who of the underworld—sitting devoutly in their seats, some of whom were now blessing themselves.

Under the rabbi's frown lay sparse brownish eyebrows, blue eyes, and a stringy beard that was either just growing in, or refused to grow at all. He stared silently at the congregation for a few minutes, put on the glasses, opened his prayer book, and mumbled Hebrew prayers in a kind of sing-song for ten or fifteen minutes with his eyes downcast, rocking slightly back and forth.

Finally he closed the prayer book and looked up at the large gathering for several moments as if trying to figure out what on earth he could say about a man such as Ben Gold. A eulogy was required. When he finally raised his voice, the tribute was boilerplate—but what else could he say? That if there was a hell Ben would be burning there, as he spoke? His sermon, at least, was short.

Then began the slow procession of cars to the Jewish cemetery for the burial. It was led by the hearse carrying Ben in his casket, followed by our limo and cars as far as the eye could see—as many as fifty or more. Arriving at the cemetery, people parked and walked solemnly in twos and threes to the burial site. There was a tent placed over the grave to protect the mourners from sun or rain or hopefully, God's wrath.

Inside the tent were more chairs. The funeral director escorted me to the middle seat of the front row. Francine, my mother, and Sam followed to places at my sides. I could smell the gin my mother had surreptitiously swigged from the flask in her purse. There weren't enough chairs under the tent for the crowd, or enough room for them to stand, so they had to remain on the grass among the already buried, with names like Goldstein, Rosen, Applebaum, Lefkowitz, carved on their tombstones. I noticed them wandering among the graves surrounding the tent, reading with interest the carved inscriptions of names, dates, and I suppose phrases like *"REST IN PEACE"* in Hebrew. Well, why wouldn't they be looking at tombstones? Death, after all, was their business.

The flower-covered casket was held up by pulleys on top of the freshly dug grave. The rabbi said the Hebrew prayer for the dead in a quick mumble and then, as a believer in conflict with his duties of burying a man like Ben Gold in the eyes of God, restlessly signaled the crowd to leave. The funeral directors leapt to their feet and herded everyone back to their cars. Sam took my arm to leave, too, but I shook it off. I wanted to watch Ben Gold being covered with dirt. Although the two grave diggers worked hard with their shovels, covering the casket took longer than I thought, and when the sky darkened and a soft rain began to fall, Sam, Francine, and my mother left to wait in the limo. But I had no intention of leaving my chair until I saw Ben Gold buried. I was bearing witness. *Bearing Witness.*

Now, sitting alone under the tent as the workers shoveled, it began to rain harder and a wind came up, slanting the rain under the tent to my face. I took off my big black hat, shook my hair loose, and let the rain fall on my face and hair. Shaking my hair out took me back to the moment I pulled off my cap revealing myself to Ben just before I shot him. Now, the rain on my face and hair felt fresh, good; the drink of life in this place of death. The workers had now covered the casket with dirt. I hurled my hat into the grave. It landed upside down and I watched as mud filled its crown and oozed out like slime. Then, I walked away.

I wrote from my journal onto these pages the story of my time with the man I called Ben Gold. I changed the names of all the characters, (including my own, for obvious reasons). It is a story. It is what happened.

About the Author

Born in Cleveland Ohio, 91 year old Babette Hughes grew up in the time of Prohibition and bootleggers. Her father was one of the first bootleggers in the country, and was murdered by the mafia in a turf war at the age of 29.

Writing has allowed her to draw from those unusual life experiences to create her characters and tell their stories (and sometimes cautionary tales) in vivid detail. Gangsters and guns, women and wine, sin and society all melded together in riveting detail for readers from all walks of life who somehow relate to the characters she creates.